MISSION BANDITS

Doc Beck Westerns Book 2

SARAH ELISABETH SAWYER

ROCKHAVEN PUBLISHING

PROLOGUE

The ringing of the chapel bells echoed across the sand floor of the New Mexican desert. The erratic clanging matched the whoops of laughter coming from men perched atop the walkway on the wall of the old adobe mission.

Sancho Guerra exited his quarters and walked over to the fountain in the center of the mission courtyard. Face shaded by his red and black felt sombrero, he enjoyed the coolness near the splashing water as he observed his men waving their guns in the air. They swept their hats off in grand gestures to welcome incoming visitors.

Both front gates were wide open and through them, Sancho could see a rickety two-wheeled cart slowly coming to the mission. Two hunch-backed men flanked the team of oxen, urging them onward, creeping along. They were old men, their lives mostly spent. Perhaps that was why they were willing to sacrifice themselves.

Two of Sancho's men fired rifle shots in the air, laughing uproariously as the two old men and the cart finally crossed the threshold and into the courtyard. They were immediately surrounded by Sancho's men, who began ripping the canvas off the cart and searching its contents.

The old men looked around, their faces scrunched and sweating. They spotted Sancho and froze.

That was good. Most people knew to fear him. He stood just under six feet tall, but it was his practiced poise that modeled his spotless red and black charro suit, its embroidered jacket, pants, and silk tie, that drew the respect he cultivated. That, along with his charming smile—a death sentence to most who met Sancho Guerra.

While two of his men maintained watch on the wall for any tricks the Mexican army or U.S. marshal in Zapata might try, the rest of Sancho's men emptied the cart of its requested contents. Under a white flag, a brave colonel of the Mexican army had asked to send in supplies to the women and children held hostage inside the mission. Sancho agreed, provided the supplies included weapons and ammunition for his men.

The headmistress of Hope Academy, Bernadette Peterson, emerged from the mission's chapel, its bells silent after his man Pinto Diaz stopped ringing them so wildly. Bernadette Peterson, an aged woman with a touch of class and dignity in her square shoulders and weathered but soft face, crossed the open ground. Sancho followed her with his eyes, but she didn't look his way. She knew how to keep herself alive in his presence, but that was as far as her respect went. He knew she didn't fear him. She was a brave, foolish gringa.

Bernadette Peterson met the two old men with a kind greeting, squeezing their hands. She said a few words to them, something that made one of the old men jerk his head up and toward Sancho with a disapproving frown. Sancho didn't move, and the old man held his gaze for a second too long.

The old man patted Miss Peterson's hand and started toward Sancho, eyes downcast, which wasn't difficult in his perpetually hunched body. When he was within ten feet of the fountain, he halted and swept his worn sombrero off and worried the rim with both hands.

"Señor Guerra, please, it is not good to starve the women and children," he said. "We brought enough food for them and for your men. We will bring more. Please let them eat until they are full."

Sancho cocked his head and spoke gently. "What is your name, please, Señor?"

"Gabino Hernandez."

"Señor Hernandez, you remind me very much of *mi abuelito*, my grandfather."

The old man raised his eyes a little, enough to meet Sancho's. "Please, señor, I am certain your grandfather would want you to treat the women and children well."

"He would."

Sancho said nothing more, and the old man shuffled back a few steps before turning and walking to the cart.

Pinto Diaz, a mountain of a man who towered above his compadres, shouted to Sancho, "There was nothing in the cart but food!"

The old men looked aghast. They hadn't expected that Sancho truly meant what he said when he agreed to allow them to bring food only if they brought ammunition and weapons, too. They thought he would show mercy.

But Sancho Guerra always meant what he said.

Pinto cocked his rifle. Most of Sancho's other twenty men stood armed around the old men, who trembled. Bernadette Peterson turned to look at Sancho, calm yet pleading. That Protestant *gringa* had much nerve.

Sancho left the coolness of the fountain and walked toward the cart. He halted, glancing between the faces of the old men whose lives were balanced on the edge of his knife.

He nodded at Pinto. "Release them, but we will keep the oxen. They will make fine *barbacoa*."

The old men looked stricken. The cart and oxen were likely intricately tied into their lives and even livelihood.

But the old men did not argue, and Pinto shouted at them to get out.

The men took a few hesitant steps backward, then turned and shuffled out the open gates. They were moving as fast as old men could.

Sancho sidestepped the cart and went to the opening of the gates. He scanned the horizon. No sign of an army waiting to launch an attack. No alert from his guards on all four walls. The old men were telling the truth. They were simply there to deliver food to starving women and children.

Señor Hernandez did remind Sancho of his grandfather.

Sancho beckoned to Pinto, who had followed him to the gates. The man understood and handed Sancho his rifle. Sancho took aim, and the double report of the rifle echoed with the screams of Bernadette Peterson.

When the dust settled, the two old men lay facedown in the desert road, bullets in their backs.

Sancho had hated his grandfather.

CHAPTER 1

It was handy having a young man to help carry luggage. It was not handy to have him arguing with Rebekah every step of the way into Zapata.

"Doc, that place ain't safe," Jimmy said, swinging her medical bag high to emphasize. She'd had gotten it repaired and refilled in Amarillo after its tribulation in the Palo Duro Canyon. She took care of it like an old friend, and it took care of her.

Her new friend, though, was more argumentative. "You heard those men talking on the train," Jimmy said. "The whole town of Zapata's been taken over. Nothing but bandits and the Mexican army fighting it out."

Rebekah sidestepped a rock in the sandy road leading into their destination, three miles from the train depot they'd departed from. "That man was drinking, and you really shouldn't listen to idle gossip, Jimmy. I appreciate your concern, I really do. But we'll be fine."

"It's not me I'm worried about." Jimmy swung the bag high. If the strap weren't new, all her glass bottles would fall right out onto the ground. "Why, if you were my ma, I wouldn't let you walk into a death trap like this."

"Your mother?" Rebekah halted, eyes wide. "Goodness, Jimmy, how old do you think I am?"

He squinted at her, even though his tan Stetson shaded his sky blue eyes from the desert sun.

"I heard it's not polite to guess a lady's age."

She couldn't help laughing. "You are a quick study, Just Jimmy."

She didn't want to add that she was, indeed, old enough to be his mother. Perhaps that was why she felt the need to finish raising him. He had much to learn, and she had no one to teach.

They finished walking the three miles to the little town of Zapata. Rebekah preferred that to riding double on Jimmy's horse or renting a buggy. After a day on the train, it felt good to stretch her legs, even with the walking they did in the Palo Duro Canyon, escaping Clem Baxter. Now it was time to do what she'd set out to do when she left Indian Territory three weeks ago. At least she hoped.

Rebekah and Jimmy entered from the north side into the deathly quiet of the town. Jimmy led the way onto the wooden boardwalk in front of the barbershop and set the medical bag and carpetbag down. He removed his hat and wiped the sweat from his forehead.

Rebekah followed, lifting her long skirt to keep from tripping. She did miss those trousers. Switching her carpetbag to her other hand helped her straighten as she looked up and down the empty street and at Jimmy, who shrugged.

"Maybe everyone's in church?" he suggested.

"It's not Sunday."

"Maybe…"

"Shh." Rebekah held up one hand and strained to listen. She heard the deep sound again. And again. It was following a steady rhythm, like a heartbeat. But this was the heartbeat of a drum.

The player came into sight at the other end of the only cross-road in town, running east to west. The drummer was a Hispanic boy wearing a long, white collared shirt leading a procession as he slowly thumped the drum. A priest and nuns followed, then a hearse.

"It's a funeral, Jimmy," Rebekah whispered, her heart bending with the palpable grief in the air.

The hearse rolled past, followed by a cart. Jimmy swept off his hat.

"A double funeral, ma'am."

He was right. The cart carried a second casket. A long line of mourners followed, led by two elderly women who clung to one another as they wept behind black veils. They were Hispanic, like most in the procession.

What had led to the simultaneous deaths of two people that draped the entire town in mourning?

Near the end of the procession was a contingent of the Mexican army in dress uniform. They kept their horses in tight, solemn rein.

Two men in western dress were on foot behind them. One glanced down the south road, the other man looked north. He spotted Rebekah and Jimmy. Startled, he eased away from the funeral procession and headed up the street toward them. The other man, younger, followed.

The sunlight caught the glint of metal from the badge pinned to the older man's silver vest. He came up to them, and Rebekah offered her hand.

"Marshal Lopez? I'm Doctor Rebekah LaRoche. I telegrammed you from Amarillo."

Marshal Lopez shook her hand, lips tight in a sad smile. "Señorita, if you had only waited for my reply, you would not have wasted the trip. Sancho Guerra and his bandits are still holding the mission captive. I fear when it is all over, there will not be anyone left alive inside."

His words chilled Rebekah as much as his delivery of them. She could tell from the flecks of gray around his temples and the experienced lines in his face that this man wasn't often wrong. He'd seen enough bad situations to know when he was facing a hopeless one.

Jimmy sighed. "I'm sorry, Doc."

Rebekah stared off toward the south where she saw the funeral procession making a swing around to the cemetery on a rise. She asked, "The mission is that direction, isn't it?"

"Sí, Señorita LaRoche," the marshal answered. "It is half a mile out of town. Two men, they went out there to take food after Sancho Guerra told Colonel Del Campo that the women and children were starving. He demanded guns and ammunition, but we sent only the food."

She asked, "The men who went, are they in the Mexican army that was at the back there?"

"No, señorita. They were the two men in the caskets."

Jimmy edged up beside Rebekah. "Doc..."

She wiped the perspiration from her forehead. "Is there somewhere we can speak that's cooler, Marshal? We walked from the train depot. I feel a little faint."

❧

IN MINUTES, they were in the marshal's office, settling into chairs. The younger man, Marshal Lopez's deputy, returned to the funeral, and Rebekah sent Jimmy to the only hotel in town to secure them two rooms and deposit their luggage.

Jimmy was reluctant to leave her but agreed when she said she would appreciate a place to rest when she finished her conversation with the marshal. She needed to find out exactly what was going on at the mission and what she could do to help.

Marshal Lopez poured two glasses of water. "It is not often I see a woman doctor."

"You've met other women doctors?"

He smiled as he handed her a glass. "Now that I think of it hard, you are the first one."

Rebekah returned the smile and accepted the water. "*Gracias.* May I ask if you know the workers at the mission well?"

The marshal sighed as he sank into the leather rolling chair behind his desk. "Miss Bernadette Peterson, she is a very fine woman. She comes to town with her children. Buys their supplies. She is adored by all." He cocked his head at Rebekah. "If I may be bold, how is it you know of her and her school?"

Rebekah took a sip of water, the liquid cooling her body and reviving her. While she was dehydrated from the walk, she still felt it was the news of the desperate situation that shook her rather than the heat, now especially at the mention of Bernadette Peterson. "My sponsor, Doctor Robert T. McKinnon in Wyoming, asked me to come and help them update their infirmary."

Marshal Lopez's face lit up. "Ah, Doctor McKinnon! He is spoken of often and fondly by Señorita Peterson. He sends much support to the school. She has considered renaming it in his honor."

Rebekah chuckled. "He would hate that."

The marshal joined her in a light laugh. "Those are the exact words of Señorita Peterson. But I have not met this Doctor McKinnon. It was kind of him to send you in his place."

There was a question in his voice, one Rebekah couldn't answer. She didn't know why Doctor McKinnon never visited the school he was dedicated to supporting.

Rebekah glanced out the window toward the south. "Tell me about this Sancho Guerra. Why is he holding the school hostage?"

Marshal Lopez's demeanor shifted. He shoved the mess of papers on his desk together, grabbed a handful, and shook them in his fist.

"These. These! All are wanted posters and warrants for the

arrest of the bandits in there. Under Sancho Guerra, they have terrorized border towns for three months, drawing the Mexican army to their trail. That pressed them north, where they left a string of destroyed homesteads of poor Mexican families, white settlers, and Indians alike. They made it to Hope Academy, the mission, late one night, baring gates that haven't been closed in years. They sent demands for money and ammunition, but the Mexican army arrived and have refused to allow us to fulfill it. I am inclined to agree with them." The marshal rubbed his eyes, drawing in a deep breath to recover from his outburst. "Once we give them what they want, they will murder those inside and leave for yet more bloodshed."

Rebekah found herself taking long, quiet breaths during the tale to remain calm. She couldn't imagine what Miss Peterson, the teachers, and the children were going through. Someone must get them out.

As if on cue, the door opened and in strode a tall man in the uniform of the Mexican army. If Rebekah recalled her military markings correctly, the gold bars on his jacket denoted his rank as a colonel.

The marshal sighed and motioned to the stalwart man. "Señorita LaRoche, may I introduce..."

The man strode to tower over her chair. "I am Colonel Del Campo, and I would ask for your cooperation in this situation, Doctor LaRoche, as I have received from your government to continue my pursuit of Sancho Guerra. You are the woman doctor sent to the school, sí?"

Rebekah was taken aback. "Why, yes, I..."

"Then you have come to help, and I will ask you to do so. You must go into the mission as planned and prepare the hostages for our attack."

Marshal Lopez jumped to his feet, sending his chair rolling into the back wall. "You will not risk more lives, Colonel! This woman is a doctor, not a spy."

The colonel squared himself with Rebekah, his eyes ablaze with determination. "Your duty is to save lives, sí, Doctor LaRoche?"

She nodded, too stunned to respond. This wasn't what she had in mind to aid Bernadette Peterson and the others.

Colonel Del Campo said, "Then I will help you perform your duty as I perform mine. We will capture, or preferably kill, Sancho Guerra before the sun sets tomorrow." He held his hand up to halt the marshal's next protest. "Lopez, I have come from the gravesides of two elderly brothers who Sancho Guerra and his men ruthlessly murdered. The women and children in the mission are being starved. I will wait no more. Better for them to perish than continue like this!"

Marshal Lopez fired back, "Colonel, your plan will cost the lives of everyone inside that mission!'

Rebekah stood to put herself between the two men, hands held up to quiet them. When they heeded, she addressed the colonel. "What exactly is the army's plan, Colonel Del Campo?"

She could tell he was pleased with her cooperation. Rebekah tried not to think too much about what he was asking.

The colonel said, "We will attack tomorrow afternoon when the sun is in the banditos' eyes. They do not believe an attack will come from the west because there is much open country. I will route Sancho Guerra and his band if it costs me every man."

Rebekah didn't move. "And what of the hostages inside?"

When Colonel Del Campo didn't answer, Marshal Lopez shook his head, and Rebekah was sure his eyes were pooling with tears. "When the guard on the western wall alerts Sancho Guerra of the attack," he said softly, "I fear he will begin killing the hostages."

Rebekah put her hand over her mouth, the full implication of what was happening sinking in.

She closed her eyes and visualized the black-and-white photograph that Doctor McKinnon kept in his office on a shelf among other photographs of friends he made during his many years of service. He once told her that his bank account could never be fuller than those faces made his heart.

Bernadette Peterson was among them.

Rebekah's mind reached back to something Doctor McKinnon had included in his letter to her about Bernadette Peterson—something unique about the woman—while she listened to the marshal and colonel argue about the proposed plan.

There was dynamite in the shed by the chapel in the mission, and the colonel was sure Rebekah could set it off on the east wall right before the army's attack and draw attention away from the hostages. She could also warn Miss Peterson and the others of the exact time of the confrontation, and they could hide. The colonel did not believe Sancho Guerra would harm Rebekah as a doctor.

Colonel Del Campo sounded confident about the whole thing, but Marshal Lopez warned that Rebekah could be killed on sight like the Hernandez brothers, even though she was a woman doctor.

Rebekah's mind went again to the black-and-white photograph.

Black and white. Now there was something.

Her eyes flew open and she began speaking before the plan fully formed in her mind, before she could think about what she was committing to.

"Marshal Lopez, could you find me a nun's habit?"

CHAPTER 2

Jimmy stared at Rebekah in disbelief. "Doc, you've gone plumb loco!"

Rebekah stood in the tiny hotel room Jimmy had secured for her. He braced both hands against the door frame as if his skinny self could block her from leaving when she was ready in her new disguise.

She watched him in the mirror as she adjusted the headpiece over her hair. "Jimmy, when this is over, we really must work on your English skills."

Jimmy stuttered, "This ain't the time for joking, ma'am! You can't really mean to ride into Sancho Guerra's fifty guns!"

"It's estimated he has twenty men. The marshal and the colonel both agreed to the plan."

"Then they're loco, too!"

Rebekah worked to make sure all of her hair was tucked under the stiff coif that framed her face, then adjusted the white wimple under her chin.

She didn't have the fortitude to argue this with Jimmy because she might back out if she did. The colonel had several encouraging points about the situation that she was clinging to, one of which was her dark skin and hair.

"They will not harm her." The colonel had sounded more confident than she felt.

But she could see the look of absolute horror on Jimmy's face reflected in the mirror. She swept the black veil around and over her head as she turned to him.

"This is not suicide, Just Jimmy," she said, her voice trembling despite herself. "We have a reasonable plan well thought out. I will go in as a nun and a medical nurse, ensuring my safety. Most of these men were raised Catholic and would not dare harm a nun. They demonstrated that on their bloody trail up to Zapata. Once inside, I can speak with Bernadette Peterson in French. That will keep me from directly communicating with the bandits. I'll use dynamite to blow up a portion of the eastern wall, convincing the bandits..."

"Dynamite!" Jimmy exploded like his own fuse had reached the end. He took his hands from the doorway and raked his fingers through his mess of sandy hair. "Doc, you can't—"

"...convincing the bandits they are under attack," Rebekah continued. "Simultaneously, Colonel Del Campo and his men will ride in from the west. With any luck, the guard will be so distracted by the explosion, the army will be through the door and on the bandits before they can harm the people inside."

Jimmy gripped his hair. "It's suicide."

"Not if I also manage to have the west gate unlocked, making the army's entrance even faster."

Jimmy worked his jaw, moving his hands to the back of his head. Rebekah could tell he was coming up with a new angle to keep the argument going.

"Ma'am, with what you just went through with the Baxters, why are you volunteering to be a prisoner?"

Rebekah paused. She recalled Doctor McKinnon's photograph

again. Her mind went to the teachers and the precious little girls trapped inside the mission.

"I must do what I can. Miss Peterson means a great deal to Doctor McKinnon, and he means a great deal to me."

Jimmy dropped his hands. "If you're bound and determined to do it, I'm going with you."

Rebekah expected this. She wound the woven belt over the black tunic. "No, Jimmy, you will not. You cannot speak French."

"I'll pretend I'm deaf. "

She smiled. "Pretend?"

"I know how to handle dynamite. You'll get both feet and your nose blown off."

"Dynamite isn't complicated, Jimmy. Colonel Del Campo is instructing me. I'll manage." She tied the belt securely. What she wanted to say next, she couldn't while looking him in the eyes. "I need you waiting for me, safe and sound when I get back. There will be much to do at the mission when this is over." She tried not to think of how full the infirmary would be when the shooting stopped, and she didn't want Jimmy there, injured or worse.

Rebekah turned back to the mirror, checking to see that she was satisfied with her disguise. There wasn't much time. Colonel Del Campo was to have a cart ready for her within the hour. He wanted her to go in right away so she could sneak the dynamite to the east wall that night.

Rebekah turned back to find Jimmy still standing in the open doorway, arms dangling at his sides, dejected. She crossed the room and reached out to squeeze one limp arm as much to strengthen herself as to encourage him.

"You are a fine friend, Jimmy," she said. "But it'll be all right. This will be all over by tomorrow night."

"That's what I'm afraid of."

Rebekah patted him again, then reached for her medical bag. He quickly grabbed it. "I'll get it loaded for you, ma'am. And Miss Rebekah?"

"Yes, Jimmy?"

"I'm not going to see you off and wish you luck. I'm going to pray for you."

Rebekah held her lips in a steady line. "I appreciate that, Jimmy."

How long had it been since she prayed?

AT THE MARSHAL'S OFFICE, Colonel Del Campo quickly briefed Rebekah on the layout of the old adobe mission and how to set the dynamite, and she finished reviewing the posters on the bandits with the marshal. The information chilled her despite the warmth of the nun's habit.

Marshal Lopez warned her to stay especially clear of a huge man with a short temper, Pinto Diaz. More than any of them, she needed to avoid the leader, Sancho Guerra. The man was wanted for multiple killings, including the assault and death of three women. He was known for his unique torture tactics.

Perhaps reading up on her enemies wasn't a good idea.

Marshal Lopez tapped her on the shoulder, startling Rebekah. She looked up at him from where she was seated by his desk. His brown eyes softened, those knowing wrinkles warning her.

"Please, señorita, know that you do not have to do this."

The deputy stuck his head through the open doorway. "Señorita, your cart, it is ready."

Rebekah stood and hesitated, fingering the large silver cross that came with her outfit. Perhaps she should do like Jimmy and say a prayer to make sure she was doing the right thing.

Instead, she answered the marshal, "I know. But I must."

She followed the deputy out and to the corner of the street where a rickety two-wheeled cart drawn by a tiny burro sat waiting. The thing hardly looked sturdy enough to carry her to the mission. She glanced at Marshal Lopez, who went to hold the animal by the harness, and raised her eyebrows.

He shrugged. "We thought it best you look as innocent as possible."

"That was wise." Rebekah admitted to herself it was the only part of this plan that was wise.

Doctor McKinnon would have a heart attack if he knew what she was about to do. But when Bernadette Peterson and the rest inside the mission were safe, he would forgive her.

Rebekah checked to see that Jimmy had placed her medical bag in the tight floorboard of the cart, then adjusted the black skirt to pull herself into the cart with Colonel Del Campo's assistance. He reminded her of the time she was to set off the dynamite: 5 p.m. the following day.

Marshal Lopez handed her the reins, though he held them an extra moment until she looked him in the eyes.

"*Dios vaya contigo*," he said. *God go with you.*

Colonel Del Campo saluted her. Rebekah nodded at both men and flicked the reins. The burro tossed her head and picked up a lively trot, heading south.

Rebekah didn't look back, having the feeling she would see Jimmy peering out from a window of the hotel or maybe from the stables at the edge of town. If she saw his torn expression again, she might lose her nerve. He was right in all his arguments.

What *was* she thinking, riding straight into the guns of murdering bandits? But she couldn't back out. She wanted to give Bernadette Peterson and the girls in the mission a tremendous hug, not attend their funerals.

❦

LONG BEFORE SHE covered the half-mile on the desert road, Rebekah spotted the mission when she topped a rise. She halted to take in the setting. No wonder it was hard for the army to get close.

From there, she could see all around the mission, exposed country for miles. On the east side, a mesa afforded protection if the army wanted to attack from there, something Sancho Guerra was prepared for.

To the west, a greater distance from the mission than the mesa, were mountain foothills that could shield the army. But once they started out, it was a long way to the mission.

The mission itself was like a fortress. The outer walls of the interior structures were connected, and a walkway around it was meant to keep watch and defend from. The chapel was distinguished with its steeple and bell tower.

The chapel was where Colonel Del Campo said the hostages were likely being held.

Fortifying herself with a deep breath, Rebekah jiggled the reins, and the little burro took off at a fast trot again, covering the stretch of flat road that would take Rebekah to the closed double gates of the mission on the north side. How was she going to get in?

She didn't need to wonder long. When she was within three hundred yards, the gates flew open and out charged half a dozen men on horseback, shouting and firing their weapons despite their lack of ammunition. They were wild, careless. Deadly.

Rebekah's stomach clenched, and her mouth went dry, ears ringing with the miniature explosions coming from the guns.

She was dead.

The bandits waved rifles and pistols in the air, along with their sombreros, laughing. They wore belts of ammunition crisscrossed on their chests. Beyond their shaggy black mustaches and occasional goatee, she recognized four of them from images on the wanted posters. Most notably, the giant man who looked like he would cut her beating heart out if he knew what she was there to do.

Still whooping, the men surrounded Rebekah's cart, kicking up dust into her eyes and mouth. She blinked, wide-eyed as she put one hand to her throat.

"Parlez-vous français?" she shouted, looking around at the men as though desperate to communicate with them.

They laughed, and one said to another in Spanish, "The sister is a little bit lost."

There were a few other comments, but from what Rebekah picked up from her limited Spanish, they did have an underlying respect for the clothes she wore.

The giant man, who Rebekah suspected was Pinto Diaz, waved demandingly toward the back of her cart. His muscles rippled threateningly under his shirt sleeves, his puny vest barely buttoning beneath his broad chest. His lips were curled in a perpetual sneer.

He barked in Spanish, "What is in here? Bombs to blow us up? Army men hiding?"

Rebekah spoke in English with a French accent. "Please, Spanish no good. Bernadette Peterson?"

The men roared with laughter, and one slapped another on the shoulder with his hat. "Her English is more worse than yours!"

The giant made hand signals like he was holding a rifle, then saluting. That was when Rebekah become certain this was one of the men Marshal Lopez warned her to avoid.

Pinto Diaz. He was missing his left thumb.

"Are soldiers hiding in your cart?" he demanded.

It was clear from the hand gestures that the man suspected Rebekah had something hidden in the cart. Thankfully, she didn't. She turned in the seat to wave her hand over the canvas covering the food and blankets the colonel had filled it with.

She said, "Food..."

Rebekah flipped back the canvas corner closest to her that was half-tucked under her seat.

Jimmy stared up at her.

CHAPTER 3

Rebekah froze. The bandits nudged their horses closer to try and get a look in the cart. Pinto Diaz leaned forward in his stirrups, straining to see what she was exposing.

Only Jimmy's sky blue eyes showed. Bags of cornmeal and beans concealed the rest of him.

Rebekah's hand shook as she pulled the canvas further off but down the cart toward the end. The shifting canvas partially covered Jimmy again. His face was tucked in the shadows of her seat, and she lowered her arm to allow the bell sleeve of her black dress to cover his eyes. She looked at Pinto Diaz, who was visually inspecting what he could see in the cart.

Another man kicked his horse around to the end of the cart and yanked on the canvas. "More supplies like this, and we can remain at the old mission until winter!"

Pinto Diaz looked hard into Rebekah's eyes, leaned back, and gave a quick jerk of his head at one of the other men.

That man let out an "Arriba!" and climb atop his saddle. He leaped off and onto the seat, rattling Rebekah, his sharp churro spurs landing right by her bare hand where she still held the reins.

Rebekah gasped as he yanked the reins from her hand, dropping into the seat beside her and whipping the burro into a flat-out run.

Rebekah clung to the seat that was suddenly far too small, holding on for dear life as the cart hit a rock in the road, bounced up on one wheel, then slammed back to the earth as they rocketed toward the open gates of the mission.

The other men followed, resuming their whooping and hollering as they escorted them in. Rebekah wiped the desert dust from her eyes in time to glance up as they passed under the gate.

She was inside. And alive. So far, so good. Except for Jimmy.

The bandit driving the cart hauled back on the reins, nearly toppling the burro that scarcely weighed as much as him. The little animal pranced to a stop, tossing her head to get relief from the bit.

Rebekah looked around the courtyard. To her right was a set of storehouses and sleeping quarters, at least according to the colonel's description of the mission layout.

Ahead was a two-tiered stone fountain, the splashing water inviting her to dip a cloth in and cool her face. The chapel was located to her left on the east wall. Beside it was a storeroom and stable attached to the adobe wall. The storeroom was where the dynamite should be. Maybe she could use the side door to slip out tonight and...

A man stepped into her line of sight, coming out of the chapel. He was square-built and held himself with an air far removed from the rest of the bandits. He wore a red and black charro suit with belts of ammunition crisscrossed over the silver embroidery of the jacket. He observed Rebekah for a long moment. Then he smiled.

Suddenly, neither her nun's habit nor being a woman doctor felt like any protection at all.

This was Sancho Guerra, terrorizer of Hope Academy.

The bandit beside her on the seat jumped to the ground, and the other men dismounted. Rebekah couldn't take her eyes off Sancho Guerra as he came slowly down the chapel steps.

Pinto Diaz quickly reported to Guerra in Spanish. Rebekah's ears and mind buzzed, thinking about Jimmy in the cart behind her and the funeral procession earlier that day.

Sancho Guerra never took his eyes off her as he listened to his man give whatever explanation he was offering for this strange arrival. Rebekah held her breath.

When Pinto Diaz finished, Sancho Guerra strolled up beside the cart where Rebekah still had a white-knuckled grip on the bench. He offered his hand to help her down.

God, help me.

Rebekah released her grip and accepted Guerra's hand. It was warm and strong as he held her steady while she climbed down from the cart. His grip was firm, even after both her feet were on the ground, causing her to meet his eyes again. He spoke in English.

"Welcome to the mission, Sister."

His voice was smooth and enticing, inviting her to trust him with her life.

"Sister! Are you all right?"

Rebekah turned at the sound of a woman's voice coming from the chapel steps. An older woman hurried down and toward them. Though Rebekah had only seen a black-and-white photo of a much younger version, she immediately recognized Bernadette Peterson. A young Hispanic girl followed behind her.

Rebekah took a deep breath and realized Sancho Guerra still had a hold of her hand. She glanced down at it and then at him, knowing the challenge in her eyes. He smiled and released her hand. This cat and mouse game with him would be delicate.

She turned back to Bernadette Peterson and melted into her arms. She whispered in her ear in English, "Play along."

Rebekah pulled back and held the woman's hands as she spoke rapidly in French. "I am Rebekah, and I am only going to speak to you in French. I have come to help get all of you out—"

Sancho Guerra cleared his throat loudly, and the women turned to him. He wiggled a finger at them as though scolding children.

"It is not polite to speak a language that others do not understand," he said gently. "You will be polite."

Rebekah glanced at Bernadette Peterson as if waiting for a translation of what he said. Bernadette squeezed her hands, then faced Guerra.

"This is Sister Rebekah. She only speaks French. We were expecting her. She came from a monastery in Paris, France, on assignment to help with the orphan children at the St. Joseph Mission. She has come here to pick up books we have in storage and bring us supplies."

Rebekah tucked those details away in her mind, although she wouldn't need them if she were to not ever speak directly to Sancho Guerra, which was her high hope. But the other men knew she could speak at least some English, and he might pressure her for a story.

At the moment, she was not sure he believed Bernadette Peterson, although the woman was so confident that Rebekah almost forgot she was speaking of Rebekah being the nun from Paris.

Sancho Guerra didn't take his gaze off her as he spoke to Miss Peterson.

"I fear you need to tell the good sister that she must delay her trip to St. Joseph's. We have need of her and her medical knowledge here."

Rebekah hadn't realized he could see her medical bag sitting beneath the bench in the cart. Did this man miss nothing?

Rebekah looked to Bernadette for translation, and the woman

spoke low in French. "Let's get you inside, and you can tell me everything."

Louder, she said in Spanish, "Josephina, will you unload the supplies that Sister Rebekah brought for us?"

Thankfully, the other men hadn't touched her cart. The young girl who had followed Bernadette Peterson from the chapel, blending into the shadow of the woman, caught hold of the burro's bridle.

Rebekah chanced saying, "Fragile. Very fragile."

She caught Sancho Guerra's gaze on her again, and she wished she hadn't spoken.

The girl, Josephina, nodded. "Sí, Sister Rebekah."

Rebekah watched the cart rumble across the courtyard toward the stable, aware of Sancho Guerra still watching her. As long as she stayed the center of attention, Jimmy was safe.

Bernadette Peterson spoke to the bandit leader. "I will take the sister inside for refreshment. She is tired from her journey."

That was so very true.

CHAPTER 4

A rattlesnake couldn't have coiled as tight as Jimmy was under the canvas in the two-wheeled cart. He heard voices when they arrived in the mission but, even though they talked in English some, he couldn't make out what they said.

He did catch something about the cargo being fragile. It was Miss Rebekah's voice. She must've directed it at one of the bandits who was now leading the cart into a stable.

Using the noise of the creaking cart to cover his movements, Jimmy drew and cocked his six-gun, holding it close to his chest. Underneath the canvas, it grew darker from the covering of a roof.

The cart stopped.

He didn't hear any footsteps. Then the canvas was drawn back. He unfurled his coil, springing to the edge of the cart with his gun right in the face of...

A little Hispanic girl?

Jimmy growled, "Who are you?"

The girl's eyes popped wide and she stared at him, but kept her mouth pressed closed. At least she hadn't screamed like most girls might when someone pointed a gun at them. Her face glowed bright even in the shadows of the barn, her long black hair done in a neat braid, tied with a blue ribbon.

Jimmy realized he still had his gun under her nose. He quickly lowered it, uncocking the hammer as he glanced around. He was inside a stable with an open front, but the cart was positioned so that the side wall blocked him from view of the courtyard. He looked to the girl and remembered a phrase Mrs. Cuesta taught him. He used it, asking the girl what her name was.

She giggled, her features relaxing. She put her hand over her mouth to muffle the sound, then said, "Señor, I understand you better when you speak in English."

Jimmy breathed a sigh of relief. "Good. I can't hardly reckon a word of Spanish."

She shook her head. "I do not know that phrase."

"Never mind. I'm just glad you're you. Thought you was one of the bandits, and I could just hear the pearly gates creaking open."

A jingle sounded, that of spurs, approaching quickly. Josephina motioned for Jimmy to get down. She quickly covered him with the canvas while uncovering the other half of the cart. The jingling stopped, and a gruff voice spoke to her, asking something. She replied quietly, respectfully, and a few moments later, the jingling sounded again as the man walked away.

Josephina peeked under the canvas. "Come, I will hide you. The men will search the cart for anything that doesn't belong to the sister. They will be here soon."

Jimmy didn't have to be told twice. He sprang out, keeping his gun in hand, landing on the dirt floor of the stable. Josephina tapped him on the shoulder and motioned toward the back corner of the stable. He followed her and found a pile of manure that made his nose crinkle.

"This where I have to stay the night?"

"Unless you prefer an open grave and the buzzards."

Her words should have sounded teasing, but they weren't. Jimmy straightened to his full height, which wasn't much to speak of, but he still overshadowed her. She didn't look afraid, though, not of him or the whole situation, despite her eyes being brown spots of sadness. But what terrible things had she seen for her to say that so solemnly?

Jimmy holstered his gun and patted her on the head. She frowned as he said, "Don't worry, little thing. Doc Beck has a plan to get you all out of here. I'm here to help."

Josephina rolled her eyes upward at where he still had his hand on her head. He took it she didn't like that and quickly dropped his hand.

"Well, anyway, I'll lay low here," he said. "I know Doc Beck isn't planning to make her move until tomorrow, but bring me word if she needs me tonight. Maybe you could bring me some food, too? Only dry goods in that cart."

He was sure the little girl was about to giggle again. Good. Looked like she needed to do just that.

CHAPTER 5

Inside the chapel, Rebekah felt like she could breathe for the first time since arriving at the mission. With the door closed, Sancho Guerra's gaze was no longer on her and her cheeks tingled as she took slow, even breaths of the stale air in the closed-up chapel.

Bernadette Peterson put her hand on Rebekah's back and guided her into the central nave, what they as Protestants would call a sanctuary. Rebekah had been in a cathedral, though it had been some time ago. It'd been some time since she'd been in any church at all.

The chancel at the front, which featured a pipe organ and altar beyond it, had been turned into a makeshift classroom. Two women were huddled with twenty students, attempting to teach a lesson. But everyone's attention turned to the nun.

One of the teachers hurried down the center aisle of the nave, looking at Bernadette questioningly.

Bernadette said quietly, "Sister Rebekah brought us supplies. Please tell the students to return to their lessons. They can speak with the sister later. She only speaks French, so I will interpret."

As the woman nodded and squeezed Bernadette's hand,

Rebekah marveled at the fine job Bernadette was doing on the fly. It was wise for them to keep up the charade even with their fellow hostages. It wouldn't do for Sancho Guerra to catch Rebekah casually conversing with one of the teachers in English.

Still, for someone who had been fluent in three languages since childhood, needing an interpreter was a new feeling for Rebekah.

Bernadette indicated one of the back pews, and Rebekah took a seat. Bernadette lowered herself beside her and took Rebekah's hands in hers again, looking her in the eye.

Though well past the flower of youth and weather-worn from years in the desert, Bernadette's skin was still flawless except for the brown spots on the back of her hands. She had elegant green-gray eyes set against her tanned skin, and she kept her salt and pepper hair up in a loose knot with natural ringlets falling to frame her face.

She said quietly in French, "You are Rebekah LaRoche, are you not?"

Rebekah nodded. "Doctor McKinnon sent me here after you requested someone to come and update your infirmary. Colonel Del Campo asked me to help with his plan to overtake the bandits."

"What is the plan?"

Before Rebekah could respond, the chapel's side door opened, and Rebekah flinched, expecting Sancho Guerra to enter the sanctuary. But it wasn't. In fact, she wouldn't have realized anyone slipped through the door if she hadn't seen how subtle Josephina was earlier. Bernadette beckoned for the girl to join them. Josephina came to stand at her side, close to the aisle.

Rebekah quickly asked in French, "Please, is the boy all right?"

Bernadette looked at her, surprised. She spoke quietly to Josephina in English, repeating the question.

Josephina nodded. "I hid him with the manure pile in the stable."

Rebekah cupped her hand over her lips, stifling a giggle. She'd like to have seen Jimmy's expression about that. He earned the treatment, though, sneaking into her cart and scaring her half to death. She was still scared for him.

Josephina asked, "May I take some bread to the young man if we have any left? He said he is hungry."

Rebekah smiled. "He is always hungry."

Josephina looked sharply at her, and Rebekah immediately realized her gaff. She had spoken in English.

Rebekah glanced to the front, where the other teachers and students were occupied in tending their lessons.

Bernadette took Josephina's other hand and drew the girl's attention. "You may as well know that Sister Rebekah is not really a nun, nor does she only speak French. She was sent to help us. But no one must know who she is nor why she is here. Do you understand, Josephina?"

Another nod and Rebekah had a feeling the girl would be better at this game than she was. She had made a mistake that cost her nothing sitting in the safety of the chapel with Josephina and Bernadette. Make the same mistake in front of Sancho Guerra, and she would be dead.

A clatter sounded at the front of the chapel, and in strode two of the bandits. One of them was Pinto Diaz.

The teachers and students ducked like turtles on a log but didn't seem overly disturbed. Apparently it was common for the men to invade the sanctuary.

The men came to the pew where Rebekah and Bernadette sat, and Pinto spoke rapidly in Spanish. Rebekah got the gist that Sancho Guerra had sent for her to care for wounded men. She held herself still and waited for the faux translation.

Bernadette spoke in French to her. "Their leader wants you to treat his men who were wounded yesterday in a shootout when the army came to recover the bodies of those two poor, blessed men, God rest their souls."

Rebekah nodded her agreement. This would be a good opportunity to scope out the sleeping quarters, which was likely a gathering place for the bandits.

And she couldn't very well refuse a request from Sancho Guerra.

CHAPTER 6

Dusk was settling as Rebekah, medical bag in hand, crossed the courtyard with the two men flanking her. She wouldn't doubt Sancho Guerra would search it. If he discovered the false bottom, she would explain through Bernadette's interpretation that she brought the pepperbox pistol for protection in the wild west. If she had a chance to speak before Guerra had her shot.

The bandit leader was nowhere in sight, not even when they entered the sleeping quarters where most of the men were. Rebekah began counting them, memorizing their faces, wanting to know how many men were there for when the action started. If possible, she needed to know where everyone was when she went to set the dynamite and unlock the west gate.

The sleeping quarters had an underlying sense of organization and cleanness that dissipated in the two weeks of the bandits making themselves at home there.

Wood pegs lined one wall where students could hang their coats and book straps. Those were cluttered with dirty sarapes and sombreros. Dusty boots littered the floor.

And the smell! Rebekah tried not to gag as she used the sleeve of her dress to cover her nose.

Pinto Diaz led her to the end of the long row of beds that the girls used while living at the mission. At the far end, two men were propped up on beds, shirtless, and boots kicked off on the floor. Despite the bandage around his midsection, the first wounded man was playing cards with a young man, a stool used as a table between them. The young man was no more than a boy, really, and quickly stood as Rebekah approached.

He held his cards in one hand as he bowed his head at her. "Sister, thank you for coming to help. I am Edgardo."

The second wounded man lay on his cot, eyes closed, snoring. Edgardo turned enough to kick the leg of that man's cot.

His eyes popped open, hand reaching for the pistol tucked under his hip. The man blinked and, seeing no danger, cursed Edgardo, wincing at the wound in his leg.

The wounded man playing cards with Edgardo leered at Rebekah, but Edgardo caught it and slapped the man's bare head.

Edgardo hissed, "The sister is here to help you, you fool. Respect her."

She heard the man mutter something about having killed a priest once.

Rebekah swallowed. Her outfit was feeling less and less protective, but it was far too late to back out of the charade. She set her medical bag on the stool beside the first wounded man. These would not be the most pleasant patients she had ever cared for.

As she opened her bag, Rebekah noted the windows lining the west wall of the sleeping quarters. From them, every bandit would have a clear view of the Mexican army's coming attack the next day. All the more reason Rebekah better make sure they were preoccupied with a massive explosion promptly at 5 p.m.

CHAPTER 7

Two hours later, Rebekah dragged herself up to the gallery inside the chapel where the hostages slept. She was hot and sticky under the nun's habit, but she knew a bath was not possible nor safe. When she left the bandits' quarters, more of them had entered, all drinking heavily. She caught talk of the whiskey running out. When it did, they'd be especially cranky.

Rebekah wanted to swing by the stables and check on Jimmy, but that wasn't possible with Pinto Diaz escorting her back to the chapel. She noted a man standing guard at the entrance and one at the side door. She'd take that into account when she slipped out to set the charge that night. Then she only had to get herself there when the time came tomorrow.

Rebekah accepted Bernadette Peterson's offer to sleep by her in the corner closest to the gallery stairs. The teachers slept nearby, and the girls slept furthest in. If the bandits charged them, the women served as a barrier to the students. At least the narrow stairwell could be defended with a single pistol, like Rebekah's pepperbox. For a short time, at least.

When they'd settled down for the night, Rebekah outlined

Colonel Del Campo's plan to Bernadette, speaking in French in case the others weren't asleep yet.

Bernadette was remarkably calm. Perhaps it was because the woman had gotten accustomed to the threat of death over them the past two weeks. But there was also a peace in Bernadette Peterson's eyes as she sat on her blanket on the floor of the gallery, sideways and propped on one hand as though they were on a Sunday afternoon picnic.

But when Rebekah mentioned slipping out to get the dynamite, Bernadette shook her head with a frown. "The dynamite is still here, but it is in the storage building by the children's sleeping quarters."

Rebekah's heart sank. "Where the bandits are quartered?"

"Yes, and no one is allowed to leave the chapel except myself and Josephina. They let her fetch us fresh water throughout the day. I don't believe they would harm her, but I keep a close eye on all my flock." She patted Rebekah's hand. "That includes you now."

Rebekah couldn't comprehend why those simple words made her heart ache. Perhaps because it had been a long time since she was truly shepherded.

But they had other matters to discuss.

"It looks as if I will need to create a small diversion to get to the bigger diversion," Rebekah said. She hesitated, not liking the idea that came to mind, but she spoke it anyway. "If Josephina could get to the storeroom, she would be able to sneak the dynamite out, wouldn't she?"

Bernadette's face paled, and Rebekah knew the woman was wrestling with the idea of putting the young girl in such danger. But they both knew none of them, including Josephina, would survive unless they did something.

"What if she is seen?" Bernadette asked.

"I will create a distraction tomorrow morning when I check on Sancho Guerra's wounded men. Instruct Josephina to be very careful and wait until I have the men's attention. Do you think she will do it?"

Bernadette smiled. "She is brave. Like you."

Rebekah sighed. "If only you had a stethoscope to my heart right now."

Bernadette's laugh was soft. "And mine."

Rebekah went through the rest of the colonel's plan, that Bernadette and the teachers were to quietly move the girls up to the gallery and barricade themselves in a few minutes before 5 p.m. They needed to buy as much time as possible if Sancho Guerra gave the order to have them killed after the attack began. She ended with the colonel's and marshal's great hope that they would all come out alive.

Bernadette sighed, the peace still on her face. "Thank you for coming to help us. It really is very brave."

"It's what Doctor McKinnon would do if he were here."

Bernadette's lips trembled. "I have no doubt he would. Did he ever tell you how we met?"

He had, but Rebekah said, "I would like to hear your version."

"It was in the Colorado goldfields," Bernadette began. "He decided to stay there a while and hunt for his fortune. He found it, but it cost him dearly. He contracted pneumonia and was alone in his cabin in the mountains with no one to care for him."

Rebekah smiled. "Except you?"

Bernadette returned the smile. "I came west with scant missionary training but convinced I could make a difference in the mining towns. The conditions were so unbelievable that my heart broke for the children I knew were being raised in them. I settled in Junction City and teamed up with the pastor and his wife there who had started a tent church."

She chuckled. "That tent served as a church, revival center, school, and hospital. He and his wife never slept. I suppose I didn't either. Several mothers joined in, and before I knew it, that camp had transformed into a real town. We were still using the tent as a hospital when they brought in Robert T. McKinnon, half-frozen and gasping for air. I'd never seen death coming on so close and quickly, and I wanted to save him in the worst way."

When Bernadette paused, Rebekah filled in with, "Doctor McKinnon said when he opened his eyes, he was confused at having an angel standing over him, wondering how on earth he made it to heaven."

Bernadette chuckled again. "Those were his very words when he regained consciousness. It was a few months before he was strong enough to leave, and we shared many good conversations and books during that time, including the Bible. I rejoiced when he accepted Jesus into his life, and I knew we would be friends for life. And we have been."

Rebekah bit her lower lip to keep from asking the question she always wanted to ask Doctor McKinnon when he told the story, gazing at Bernadette Peterson's photograph. He never went beyond that part of the story nor explained why their friendship had remained letter correspondence and his contributions to the school.

Bernadette Peterson didn't go on either.

She patted her blanket, shifting the mood. "I have always wanted to meet you, Rebekah. When Robert told me how you had graduated medical school and were doing such good work among the Omaha, I knew you were a fine young lady. I had no idea he would send you here to us."

Rebekah held her composure at the mention of her people, the ones she had left behind on the Omaha Reservation in Nebraska. This wasn't the time or place to go down that road. Her heart ached enough.

When the silence stretched, Bernadette said quietly, "I met John LaRoche and his wife not long after they married, and I knew he had a heart of gold."

Rebekah nodded. "So I've heard."

Bernadette looked surprised at the detached tone of

Rebekah's voice. But Rebekah hadn't known John LaRoche, missionary to the Omahas, nor was she related to him as most people thought.

Her father had been such a great admirer of the man, he took the name LaRoche as his own. That caused confusion about Rebekah's parentage, but it didn't matter. Few people outside of Doctor McKinnon knew her whole story, and she would rather keep it at that.

It was the way of the west, to live life that day and going forward without constantly looking over your shoulder. That was how Rebekah's heart survived.

Bernadette reached out and patted Rebekah's cheek. "I hope you sleep well tonight, my dear. I have a feeling tomorrow will be quite a day for all of us."

CHAPTER 8

Early the next morning, Rebekah barely finished her breakfast—a small bowl of rice like the rest of the hostages—when Pinto Diaz and the polite boy, Edgardo, came to escort her to the sleeping quarters. Rising from the table in the kitchen that adjoined the chapel, Rebekah caught Bernadette Peterson's gaze. She shifted her own to include Josephina.

It was time to set their plans in motion.

Outside, Rebekah breathed deeply as they crossed the courtyard. She wanted to fill her lungs with fresh air before entering that hideous place.

Before they reached the door, the back of Rebekah's neck began tingling. She looked around. Sancho Guerra watched her from the dirt porch of Bernadette Peterson's quarters that he occupied. He casually leaned back against a support post, dressed in a cream charro suit, thumbs hooked in his adorned metal belt.

Even in the relaxed position, he looked deadly. He tipped his bare head in salute at Rebekah.

She faced forward again, grateful for the stiff coif and black veil that partially concealed her face.

Several of the men were still lounging on their cots, hungover from last night. She wished she could signal Colonel Del Campo that this was the time to attack.

She treated her two groggy patients along with three other men—one suffering from blistered feet, another with a roaring headache, and the third a festering splinter. That last one asked if she could take his confession, but she pretended not to understand him.

He muttered under his breath, sounding like he was confessing anyway as Rebekah extracted the splinter with her tweezers. She cleaned the infected area with whiskey from the bottle on the table. He took a swig, too. The bottle was almost empty.

When she finished with the man's hand, Rebekah started cleaning and replacing her instruments in her medical bag, taking her time. She glanced at Edgardo, who was supposed to be guarding her, but he was talking with a man near the door.

Keeping her movements inconspicuous was easier with the flowing sleeves of her black dress. She took up her medical bag and moved as though to leave but sidestepped to the cabinet where two whiskey bottles were left. She slipped one off the shelf and into her half-open bag, turned, and strode for the door.

Edgardo moved as if to lead the way out, but she pushed past him and to the long dirt porch outside the sleeping quarters. Two men leaned against the building, whittling and talking. The door to the storage building was in plain view of at least six men now.

She glanced to her left to see Josephina lingering near the front gates and the door, slowly stacking wood in her arms for the kitchen stove. Rebekah caught her eye, and Josephina blinked long. The girl was ready. Was Rebekah?

She stepped out from under the overhang and dropped her medical bag with a thud, drew out the whiskey bottle, and wheeled around to face Edgardo and the other man who had followed her out. This was going to attract more attention than she wanted, but only a big show could guarantee Josephina wouldn't be seen.

Rebekah pointed an accusing finger at the men. "Drink! Sin!"

The bandits looked taken aback, their rifles dangling casually. A third man stepped outside to see what was going on.

Rebekah shrieked louder, "Drink! Drink! Sin! Sin!"

From the corner of her eye, she saw the guards above the front gate turning to look at her. She hadn't needed to get their attention, but at least they couldn't see the front door of the storeroom below them. Two other men who had been loitering by the storage building, smoking, straightened and cocked their heads at the crazy French nun waving her arms and wagging a finger at the bandits.

Rebekah gave another shout of "Sin!" before upending the whiskey bottle, the liquid hitting the dust and sending up mud droplets.

The man with Edgardo yelled and lunged for her, but she spun away, keeping the bottle out of his reach as she continued to pour it. The men leaned on the sleeping quarters' wall hollered, and sprang forward.

Almost instantly, Rebekah was surrounded by a dozen bandits, including ones who stumbled out of the quarters, still feeling their hangovers. Most importantly, the ones near the storeroom hurried over.

Rebekah stopped pouring, not wanting to arouse too much anger too suddenly. Right now, the men were howling in disbelief, but none of them dared attack her.

She swung the bottle through the air in a circle while she screamed at them. "Sin, sin!"

As she made her turn, she saw Josephina edging close to the storeroom door, her thin arms holding three chunks of wood. Rebekah turned her back, hard as it was, and focused on keeping the bandits' attention. She shook the bottle at them and upended it to let another quarter of the bottle spill out.

One of the men fell to his knees in front of her, clasping his hands together in a pleading gesture. "Sister! Sister, please, no sister."

Rebekah glared at him. Then suddenly, all of the men went silent. There was no sound save for the liquid splashing on the ground.

Sancho Guerra stepped into the inner circle with Rebekah. She slowly leveled the bottle to stop the spill as her heartbeat doubled.

He looked far calmer than Rebekah knew he was. Certainly more than she. He was facing her, able to see right over her shoulder and to where Josephina was close to the storage building.

But Sancho Guerra wasn't looking over her shoulder, at least not at that moment. He shook his head, tsk-tsking as he spoke in English.

"Sister Rebekah, this is not a good thing you do. My men have suffered much these past weeks, and they need more comfort than a clanging chapel bell gives them." He held out his hand. "Please, you will give me the bottle now."

Rebekah didn't move. She held the bottle level in her hand. If she defied him, she risked losing the relative freedom she'd been given in the mission. She could lose her life.

From far behind her, the storeroom door creaked.

Rebekah tilted the bottle to let the last of the whiskey pour out on the ground. No one moved or spoke as the last drop fell.

Rebekah held her chin as steady as she could. "Sin."

She handed the empty bottle to Sancho Guerra, feeling the hot anger radiating off his body as he took the bottle, his eyes never leaving her face. If he felt any kinship with her dark skin or compassion for her nun's habit, it didn't show.

For another long moment, no one moved. Then Sancho Guerra took a step back, turned, and, holding the bottle by its neck, smashed it into a support post.

Two men jumped back, covering their faces against the flying shards of glass.

Sancho Guerra turned back to Rebekah, still holding the neck of the bottle with its jagged ends catching the morning sun.

Rebekah knew precisely how much damage a broken glass bottle could do. She had stitched up more than one man's face after a saloon fight.

Sancho Guerra stepped toward her, and Rebekah involuntarily took a step back. She wanted to flee, but she had to keep his attention. Where was Josephina? Was she out of the storeroom yet? Was she even able to find the dynamite?

These questions flashed through Rebekah's mind like the final moments of her life should have as Sancho Guerra lifted the whiskey bottle to chest level. She recalled reading about how he enjoyed torturing his victims before taking their life.

He moved another step toward her and pressed against her cheek with one point of the sharp glass. Then he lifted the bottle and swung it over her nose to touch her other cheek. Rebekah closed her eyes.

Sin.

The sharp piece pushed against her soft flesh. She kept her eyes squeezed shut, not wanting Sancho Guerra to have the pleasure of seeing the pain in them when he stabbed her.

But he didn't. The cold sharpness lifted away from her face, and Rebekah opened her eyes to find him inches from her.

The sound of the chapel door opening across the courtyard broke the moment. Rebekah heard footsteps running across the courtyard, and in a moment, Bernadette Peterson was at her side, clutching her arm and speaking in French.

"The girl got it. Come inside where it is safer."

Rebekah let her breath out, realizing she was leaned back on her heels as far as she could without falling. She let the strong older woman hold her steady as she guided her out of the circle of men.

Would Sancho Guerra choose to kill Rebekah that morning, or could she stall him until the army attacked at 5 p.m.?

⚜

AS SOON AS they were inside the chapel, Rebekah whispered to Bernadette, "Did Josephina put the dynamite by the wall?"

Bernadette took her by the arm and led her to the side of the alcove. "She could not. One of the men nearly saw her. She hid it in the stable with the boy you brought."

Rebekah chewed her lower lip. "Please give her a message to pass on to Jimmy. He is to work with Josephina to get the dynamite to the wall before 5. She can keep watch while he lights the fuse." *If he can.* Rebekah earnestly hoped Jimmy hadn't been spinning a yarn when he said he could handle dynamite.

She continued, "Have Jimmy time the explosion to go off at precisely 5. A few minutes before, I will go to the west gate and unlock it."

"This is very dangerous, as was what you did out there."

"Be that as it may, this is a desperate situation, Miss Peterson."

Bernadette took both her hands and squeezed them. "Be careful, child. I will have everyone locked in the gallery at 5."

CHAPTER 9

The dynamite was old and had begun to sweat in the closed-up storeroom. Those scoundrels didn't know a hoot about dynamite, moving it from one building to another and not bothering to cover it with hay to keep the sticks and blasting caps cool.

It was good that Jimmy did know about dynamite and that he had hay handy to make a bed for the small box Josephina tossed at him as she darted back out of the stable before she was seen.

The fact that Jimmy was a good catch kept them both from being blown to kingdom come.

As the morning wore on, so did Jimmy's nerves, packed between the manure pile and the sweating dynamite. Near lunchtime—boy, he was hungry—Jimmy pulled the box from the hay and examined it. The box had blasting caps and fuses with the seven sticks of dynamite. Dynamite was a stable explosive but not rotting stuff like this. Whoever donated it to the church knew to get it off their property and used soon. That was exactly what Jimmy intended to do.

"It is good?"

Jimmy nearly dropped the dynamite at the nearness of

Josephina's voice. She stood at the corner of the stall that the manure pile and Jimmy were tucked in.

How could he have not heard her approaching? Of course, his senses weren't all that great, but still. This girl moved with the stealthiness of a mountain cat. But she was gentle looking.

Jimmy raised from where he had been squatted by the hay with the dynamite. "It'll do. What was all the ruckus out there earlier?"

"Sister Rebekah was causing a distraction for me to get the dynamite."

"Must have been some show."

"It was."

Jimmy pulled out his pocket knife and knelt by the dynamite again. He measured the fuse to give him five minutes to get clear. More or less. "What time am I supposed to touch off the dynamite?"

"Touch off?"

"Blow up the wall."

"Oh. The sister said 5. It will draw the guards' attention."

"So she hopes." Jimmy frowned. "You got a watch?"

Josephina nodded. "Señorita Bernadette gives me one."

"Good."

Josephina came into the stall and squatted beside him, hands on her knees as she watched him recheck the length of the fuse.

"Why did you come with Sister Rebekah against her wishes?" she asked.

Jimmy cut the fuse cleanly, then reached for a blasting cap. He inserted it into one of the sweating sticks. Slow and steady. "I knew she needed my help, but that she was too stubborn to let me do anything."

"It was a very dangerous thing you did," Josephina said softly. "If Sancho Guerra's men see you in the cart, they kill you both."

Jimmy nearly fumbled the stick and cap. He regained control and gently laid the finished stick back on the bundle. He began threading the fuse into the blasting cap. "I guess I didn't think about that. I just knew I couldn't let her come in here alone. Especially handling dynamite. She can do a lot of things, but this requires a special touch."

"You are very close to her?"

Jimmy shrugged, but he decided to say what was stuck on his tongue to say. "You ever have someone care about you? I mean, truly care about you as a person, for who you are and who you could be, not just as another human being to be nice to?"

"Señorita Bernadette is for me."

"Well, Doc Beck is that way for me." Jimmy finished threading the fuse and laid the stick with the others. "She's like a Christmas present God wanted to give me that I've been waiting for my whole life."

Josephina nodded. "I understand this, Señor Jimmy."

He chuckled. "It's just Jimmy."

He tied the seven sticks of dynamite together, his movements slow and easy. Then he looked Josephina straight in the eye. "This dynamite is touchy. You better stay in the chapel at five."

Josephina shook her head. "I am to help you place the dynamite and keep watch while you light it. I know every crack within these walls, all of Sancho Guerra's men and their habits. I will get you there."

"It's too dangerous."

"It is more dangerous if you are not successful."

She had a point. Jimmy tapped the air above the dynamite. "Let me tell you a few things about this dynamite, then. You know, in case anything happens to me. It could be left up to you, Josephina."

She nodded solemnly. Since the first time she smiled at his attempt to speak Spanish, he hadn't seen this girl crack a smile, not even when she brought him breakfast, and he said her eyes were just like a little fawn's. He couldn't recall smiling much himself since being inside the mission. That would come later when they were celebrating freedom from Sancho Guerra's men.

But he knew those men weren't going down without a fight. There would be dead men on this day. Hopefully, it wouldn't be the good guys.

CHAPTER 10

Rebekah was disrupted from joining the teachers and girls for the noon meal by Edgardo. He was to fetch Rebekah to come take the meal with Sancho Guerra.

She stood stock-still in the doorway leading to the kitchen, trying to pretend she didn't hear what she'd just heard. Bernadette Peterson was nearby to translate the Spanish words as Edgardo waited, his face pinched and lips pale. Did he know what Sancho Guerra intended?

Instead of translating his words, Bernadette Peterson said in French to Rebekah, "Be careful, my dear. Their leader is very angry with you. Please do what you can to smooth it over. It is still a long way until 5."

Rebekah nodded as though she was just receiving the initial message. She meant it for Bernadette's wise words as well. She overdid it in the courtyard during her face-off with Sancho Guerra, but she didn't regret it. Anything less, and he would have seen Josephina slipping out of the storeroom with the dynamite, and the girl would have had the glass bottle pressed into her face instead of Rebekah.

Edgardo led Rebekah to Bernadette's quarters, taken over by

49

Sancho Guerra. Edgardo halted on the dirt porch and looked at Rebekah, a hesitant apology in his eyes. She recalled how he rebuked the wounded man for something he said about priests and nuns.

This boy must have been raised a devout Catholic. Perhaps he even held to some of his beliefs despite his current associates. Rebekah didn't recall a bandit named Edgardo among the warrants at Marshal Lopez's office. He had no murder accusations hanging over his head. Yet.

Edgardo motioned for her to go inside, making it clear he wasn't going in. Rebekah left him on the porch, though she had a sincere wish that he would go inside with her.

The interior of the adobe dwelling was dim but fragrant with the scent of a hearty meal. Even the smell of beef! The hostages were fortunate to have rice and enough cornmeal to make a few tortillas.

When her eyes adjusted to the dimmer interior, Rebekah recognized the simple quarters of a humble woman. It was comfortably but sparsely furnished. Over the white adobe fireplace was a mantle and Rebekah found herself drawn to it. Center on the mantel was a black and white photograph of a younger Doctor Robert T. McKinnon.

"Sister Rebekah. Come."

Rebekah jerked and looked to her left, where tan linen curtains disguised a doorway into an alcove. Through the linen, Rebekah discerned Sancho Guerra standing at the head of a small table with a feast spread before him. He beckoned at her. "Come, sister."

Rebekah gave herself a quick mental reminder that she must pretend to understand very little of what he said and be very, very cautious. Sancho Guerra was already suspicious of her, made worse by the display with the whiskey bottle.

As Bernadette said, it was a long way to 5 p.m.

Rebekah used both her hands to part the split in the linen

curtains and halted in the doorway, trying to assume a humble expression. Sancho Guerra indicated the bench seat to his right. She imagined Bernadette using the table to host her students and teachers for warm meals and pleasant conversations.

There was a warmth and pleasantness in Sancho Guerra's gaze that made Rebekah's mouth go dry.

Rebekah lowered herself onto the end of the bench furthest away from him. That didn't satisfy him. He waved her closer, toward the middle of the bench where a plate, fork, and knife was set.

She scooted down, mindful of her nun's habit and hoping he was, too.

Sancho Guerra reached for a flat basket and opened it to reveal steaming tortillas. Had he prepared the meal himself, or did he have a cook that already left? There was no sound of anyone else in the house.

He offered the basket to her, but when Rebekah didn't move, he peeled one tortilla out and flipped it onto her plate. This close and with the light streaming through the one window in the alcove, Rebekah noted how clean and manicured Sancho Guerra's fingernails were. It spoke of a gentleman who should be residing in a fine hacienda on some large rancho. Maybe he did, when he wasn't out killing elderly men.

Sancho Guerra indicated barbecued meat on the platter before her. She moved slowly to take a piece and add it to her tortilla. There were also tamales, chiles, rice, and beans—a true feast in this place—but Rebekah began rolling the tortilla to indicate that was all she wanted. Hopefully, he would think it was because of her humility as a nun.

In truth, Rebekah wouldn't mind a steak dinner when this was over.

Sancho Guerra turned his attention to making his own plate with all of the trimmings. He rolled the meat and sauces in a tortilla and pressed to seal it. Then, to her surprise, he took up a knife and fork to cut it with.

After chewing his first bite and swallowing, he said in English, "Sister Rebekah, you are a most intelligent woman. You have traveled a great distance from your homeland in France to help poor children in New Mexico Territory."

He cut another piece then paused to observe her. She appropriately reacted when he said *France* and *New Mexico* because, of course, she would recognize those words. How much could she pretend to understand without giving herself away? She took a bite of her modest tortilla and swallowed with the help of the mug of water by her place setting.

Was she behaving like a nun? Would a real sister decline the food and begin packing it up to take to the hungry girls in the chapel? That was certainly what this Sister Rebekah wanted to do, but she kept Bernadette's words in mind. She had antagonized Sancho Guerra enough for one day, and one day was all she had.

He took another bite, chewing slowly. He didn't speak with his mouth full, another trait of a gentleman so unlike what Rebekah witnessed among his men.

Could he sense how excruciatingly uncomfortable Rebekah was? He seemed to take delight in dragging out every moment. At least she did have training in sitting for hours, listening to elders share stories of her people. This already felt like hours, though, and not near the comfort of home. How she wished she were there!

Rebekah took another bite, hoping she wouldn't choke. She shouldn't be eating at all for risk of vomiting, but it gave her something to do and also was in obedience to Sancho Guerra. It was a cat and mouse game like she had never played before in her life.

Sancho Guerra took a drink from his mug. Wine? How much was he accustomed to drinking? If only he got drunk and stupid like his men. But he seemed in control of his senses. For the moment.

It unnerved Rebekah how he could do anything, including eating, without taking his eyes off her. Was this one of his torture techniques? It felt so. Rebekah was becoming dizzy from the pressure of it.

"Sister, it was not a good thing you did this morning," he said. "My men, they think too much of what you are. I concern myself only with *who* you are."

He leaned back in the chair and wiped his mouth with a cloth napkin. "And I feel who you are, Sister Rebekah, is not Sister Rebekah."

She kept herself still, trying not to show emotion on her face. If she did only speak French, she would have picked up little except her name. She cocked her head as though wishing she could understand what he said.

Sancho Guerra didn't move for a moment, then folded his hands over his trim midsection. His charro jacket was rich and finely made—a custom fit.

"That colonel, he is a very clever man," he said. "He thinks he will kill me in this place, but he will not. He knows nothing of Sancho Guerra. Just as you know nothing of him, Señorita Rebekah."

Warning bells clanged in Rebekah's mind like a fire wagon rocking through her. In a few simple words, Sancho Guerra had taken apart the plan and handed it back to her in pieces. And he called her señorita, not sister.

But he was bluffing. As long as Rebekah could maintain a strong charade, he wouldn't know whether he was right.

Taking another drink of water to steady herself, she looked Sancho Guerra in the eyes and spoke in French. "May God have mercy on your soul." In English, she added, "I pray...for you."

She could tell from the humorous glint in his eyes that he didn't believe her. It wasn't a very good lie. She had no intention of praying for Sancho Guerra, except perhaps that God would send him straight to hell that day.

Rebekah indicated her empty plate. "*Merci.* Gracias." She awkwardly scooted to get around the bench in the nun habit.

By the time she made it up, straightening her black dress and belt, Sancho Guerra was on his feet and standing in the curtained doorway. The only other doorway led into a darkened room—Bernadette Peterson's bedroom where he slept.

Sancho Guerra let his arms hang casually at his sides, something he did often. He was ready to strike whenever he felt like it.

"Señorita, I sense you are lying to me," he said, his voice hardening. "I have no patience with liars."

Rebekah kept her gaze lowered, determined to keep up her façade that she didn't understand what he was saying. Something bubbled out of her lips in French, something about asking him to please excuse her, to let her return to the chapel.

Her words needed no translation. He knew what she was asking, but he didn't move.

Panic seized Rebekah's heart, but she forced herself to breathe slow and wait. It was Sancho Guerra's move.

And he did move, taking a step toward her. "You wear no rosary in your belt to protect you." He slid his hand through her woven belt and gripped it.

Rebekah jerked back and slapped him. She gasped, her hand stinging from the blow and the shock of what she'd done.

Before she could think, Sancho Guerra released her belt and backhanded her, sending her stumbling over the bench and crashing into the table.

The table scraped the wood floor with a shriek as it slid away. Rebekah tumbled to the floor. Sancho Guerra grabbed her arm and yanked her to her feet.

A rip sounded as Edgardo tore through the linen curtains in the doorway.

"Please, Papá, no! Please do not harm the sister."

Everything stilled in the room, Sancho Guerra's hot breath pouring over Rebekah as he held her close. She stared at Edgardo, shocked at what he said. Was this boy really Sancho Guerra's son?

She trembled, having no sense of how she could continue her façade. She tried to straighten her black veil and white coif over her stinging cheek. She felt warm liquid at the corner of her lips. Blood.

Sancho Guerra stared at Edgardo for several seconds before releasing Rebekah. He took a step back and made a grand gesture toward the doorway.

Rebekah didn't hesitate. She shot out of the alcove, through the living room with its photograph of Doctor Robert T. McKinnon on the mantel, and out the open front door.

She ran across the courtyard and straight into the chapel, letting the door bang into the wall. She came to a halt when she entered the sanctuary, aware of the students and teachers at the altar, staring at her.

One of the teachers hurried forward. Rebekah backed away, turned, and fled up the stairs to the gallery. She found Bernadette Peterson there, on her knees by her makeshift bed on the floor, hands clasped and tucked under her chin.

Bernadette looked up at Rebekah. "I was praying for you..."

She halted and quickly stood. Rebekah swept off the disheveled coif and veil and dropped them to the floor. Bernadette said nothing, just pulled Rebekah into a tight hug.

It wasn't until she was in Bernadette's arms that Rebekah began to shake uncontrollably. Physical shock was setting in.

If she were the doctor and not the patient, she would tell herself to take several deep, slow breaths. Instead, she held on when Bernadette started to pull back.

The older woman held her close until the trembling passed.

CHAPTER 11

They were the most tedious minutes of Jimmy's young life, carrying sweating dynamite through the mission's shadows a half-hour before 5 p.m. Josephina instructed him that in order to get to the end of the east wall, they needed to stay underneath the guard walkways. But there was one place that they would have to cross into the open where a long workshop jutted out from the wall. They would go in the side door, but then they would have to go out the front window and scramble back to the wall.

Jimmy didn't like the idea of climbing through a window in a hurry toting sweating dynamite, with more eyes around than in a sack full of potatoes. But Josephina seemed to know what she was doing.

Jimmy stayed crouched in the shadows under the guard walkway by the workshop. He could hear the man's boots as he passed over, making his slow, lazy walk that the bandits assumed when they were keeping guard. He got the sense that none of them liked guard duty. Really, they didn't seem to like much of anything except drinking after being cooped up in the mission for two weeks. They were like the sweating dynamite Jimmy kept curled under one arm and supported with his other hand.

It rankled him that he could look across the courtyard and down aways to the west gate that needed to be unlocked, and he couldn't do it. A bar held it fast and would surely be noticed if it went missing. He couldn't chance tipping off the bandits.

Josephina eased open the side door of the workshop and motioned Jimmy forward. He ran through the door, still crouched.

The inside of the place wasn't much with its musty smell, but it sure beat the manure pile he'd been keeping company with.

He followed Josephina around broken furniture stored there in need of repairs. They reached the front window, and Jimmy was dismayed to see that it was right across from where Sancho Guerra was headquartered. If the man stepped outside at the wrong moment, Jimmy was a cooked goose.

There was no glass in this window, only the shutters that hung open. Jimmy realized Josephina must've opened them at some point to prepare for their adventure.

She whispered, "Stay here. I will go around and make sure no one watches. I will make the sound of a warbler, and you should come. "

Jimmy felt stupid, but he had to ask, "What's a warbler?"

Josephina smiled a little. "My papá taught me many sounds for birds. There are no red-faced warblers inside the mission today, but you will know its sound."

Josephina went back out the side door, closing it silently behind her. Jimmy waited, sweating bullets like the dynamite under his arm.

Within two minutes, he heard the trill of a bird, so lifelike he was sure it was an actual bird and not his little friend. But when it sounded again, closer to the window, he knew that was the signal.

Jimmy climbed out of the window, landed on both feet, and darted for the other side of the building. He didn't breathe until he was in the shadows again. He looked for Josephina, and suddenly she was beside him.

"Come," she whispered. "We are almost there."

They darted behind a stack of empty crates, and there was the section of wall they needed to blow up—right across from the west gate. Jimmy would have picked a different spot, but the wall was half gone and was far enough from the chapel to draw the bandits well away from there.

Not far from the sagging wall was an empty hog pen with fairly fresh mud. Those bandits scavenged anything edible in the mission.

Jimmy took another look at the wall and gave a satisfied nod. The amount of dynamite he had would give those bandits plenty to think about.

He took an empty crate from the back of the pile and carefully arranged the dynamite inside to disguise it. Burned-out cigarettes littering the area told how the bandits hung around there.

Jimmy started laying out the fuse, stringing it toward the shelter of the crates. But the hair on the back of his neck stood up. He halted then caught sight of Josephina motioning him behind the crates. He slipped behind them just as two of Guerra's men walked by not twenty feet away.

The bandits halted. One of them, the biggest man Jimmy had ever seen, produced a pouch of tobacco. He was missing his left thumb but didn't have any trouble rolling a cigarette. The bandits stood awhile, smoking and chatting.

Jimmy gritted his teeth. The men were awful close to the crate with its sweating dynamite. One burning bud flicked close to the blasting cap could set it off and blow them all to kingdom come.

He wouldn't mind seeing those men caught in the blast, but he and Josephina would get it, too. Plus, if the dynamite went off too soon, it wouldn't do the Mexican army or the hostages any good.

Jimmy leaned back on his heels to whisper in Josephina's ear, "Whatever happens, you stay out of sight, you hear?"

She didn't nod, her eyes frozen wide open. He looked back quickly to see the big bandit, cigarette in hand, twisting around and staring intently at the stacked crates. He flipped the cigarette away, still red hot, toward the crate where the dynamite was.

Jimmy was about to be spotted.

He gulped, dashed out, and grabbed the cigarette, then made a beeline for the empty hog pen. The man shouted as Jimmy leaped the low fence. He pretended to trip and went sprawling in the mud. A shot sounded right when he landed face down in the muck.

He shook the mud from his eyes and heard laughter close behind him. The big man hopped into the pen, landing on Jimmy's hand. Jimmy winced, sure it was broken. The man pushed Jimmy facedown in the mud. He went deep, the muck filling his mouth, nose, and ears.

Jimmy kicked his feet then stilled, hoping the man would think he'd passed out.

When he thought he really would pass out, the man hauled Jimmy up by the collar and the back of his belt while the other man opened the corral gate. Jimmy spat mud and gasped. He twisted, trying to free himself, feeling like a fish on a hook as his arms and legs met nothing but air.

The big man started parading with Jimmy, where the shot and laughter had drawn the whole stinking gang to the middle of the courtyard.

The man shouted something in Spanish, something about fish. He had that right. Jimmy was a fish on a hook, and there was no getting off it.

CHAPTER 12

The sound of a gunshot inside the adobe walls and the ensuing mayhem drew Rebekah and Bernadette from the chapel, where they were hovering in the alcove. It was nearly 5 p.m., and Bernadette instructed the teachers to have the children in position to dash to the gallery as soon as the explosion happened.

Rebekah was just ready to make her exit out the side door to try and reach the west wall undetected when the shot sounded. Her mind immediately went to Jimmy and Josephina, knowing they were out placing the dynamite.

As soon as Rebekah stepped onto the porch of the chapel—coif, wimple, and veil secured firmly—she saw Pinto Diaz near the fountain, holding Jimmy aloft and shouting in delight. Jimmy was covered from head to toe in mud, flailing like a turtle on its back.

Rebekah lost her breath and started down the steps, wondering if her nun habit would be enough to rescue Jimmy from the bandits. Where was Edgardo?

Just then, Sancho Guerra stepped into the doorway of his quarters and took in the sight. And her. Rebekah froze.

Pinto Diaz dunked Jimmy in the fountain, then flipped him

out and onto his feet. The big man kept a secure hold on the back of Jimmy's collar and britches, leaving the boy to swing his fists in a fruitless effort to hit the man.

The bandits formed a circle, enjoying the exhibit. Rebekah glanced up to see the guards on the walkways facing toward the courtyard, not the outer walls. The army would attack in minutes, but this wasn't the major distraction the colonel planned. Not one that would cost a human life.

Sancho Guerra entered the circle and came to stand in front of Jimmy, who immediately stilled. The poise of the bandit leader always commanded respect.

The circle hushed, though the bandits were still grinning. Sancho Guerra cocked his head at Jimmy. "And where did you come from, young *gringo*?"

Jimmy barked, "You fellers aren't the only ones that know how to steal food! I've been holed up in this mission for weeks, right under your nose."

Rebekah knew it pained Jimmy to outright lie, but he was convincing at least. He was a good storyteller, though she wasn't sure this tale would save his life.

Sancho Guerra swung his gaze around to Bernadette Peterson, who remained silent. It wasn't necessary for her to confirm or deny Jimmy's story. He could have hidden in that mission without her knowledge.

Instead of lingering on Bernadette, though, Sancho Guerra fixed his gaze on Rebekah. Her trembles started again. She'd never known a man to have the power to instill such fear in her with only his eyes. And he was well aware of that power.

He turned back to Jimmy. "Well, young gringo, there is not enough food for the mouths we have. I am afraid we must kill you."

One of the men stepped forward, drawing out a Bowie knife. He spoke in English as though to strike more fear. "Let me cut out his tongue and skin him alive."

Rebekah gasped, knowing from reading the warrants that it wasn't a figure of speech.

She rushed into the circle and in front of Jimmy, spreading her arms wide, hoping her long black sleeves and white coif would hold sway with these men as it had with the whiskey bottle. If only the marshal hadn't forgotten a rosary for her belt, she would wave it wildly now.

She looked pleadingly at Bernadette and shouted in French, "Tell them it is a great sin to take an innocent life! Tell them they will go straight to hell today if they do. Tell them anything to make them stop!"

Rebekah was aware of the tears streaking down her dusty face.

Behind her, Jimmy whispered, "Don't, Miss Rebekah."

Sancho Guerra looked at his man with the knife and back at Rebekah. She was sure he was contemplating ordering the man to skin her alive, too.

She wasn't the only one who understood that look. From outside the circle, Edgardo pressed forward to his father. "It is better to keep the hostages alive, is that not what you said? We can whip the boy and send him out with a message that Colonel Del Campo would understand."

It wasn't a very convincing speech, but there was something about it that made Sancho Guerra flick his wrist at the big man. "Lock the young gringo in the corn crib. We will roast him later."

Sancho Guerra's gaze swept to Rebekah as she lowered her arms, swallowing and shifting her gaze to Edgardo.

That was a mistake. She knew it in the way that Sancho Guerra stiffened. He would not tolerate anyone interfering with the respect his son should have for him.

CHAPTER 13

For all the anticipation of the moment, everything was happening too fast for Rebekah.

Jimmy was taken away, and Bernadette Peterson ushered Rebekah back into the chapel. The teachers and girls stood anxiously in the foyer, not certain what to do. It was 5 p.m.

Rebekah slipped her hand into the slit of her dress that she created after her fight with Sancho Guerra. She withdrew her pepperbox pistol from her undergarments and handed the gun to Bernadette.

"If anyone comes up the stairs, shoot them."

The way Bernadette took the pistol told Rebekah it wasn't the first time she'd handled a gun. Rebekah hated to be unarmed, but she didn't know if she would be able to fulfill the task of lighting the dynamite and getting to the west wall before the Mexican army attacked, and the hostages needed protection.

Rebekah dashed to the side door of the chapel, hoping the guard for it was still out front in the courtyard where she had last seen him. She peeked out the door and saw him walking her direction.

She watched with the door almost closed. Someone called to him, and he paused to look back. Rebekah bolted through the door, not bothering to close it behind her. He would look inside first and think the wind had blown it open, giving her a few precious more seconds.

Rebekah hurried inside the open stable and hid behind the cart. The man went to the side door of the chapel, peered inside, then looked around quickly. He didn't spot her and closed the door with a thump.

Rebekah swallowed and stole around the cart, making her way to the other side of the stable. Once out, she followed the pathway that Josephina described for her to get from the chapel to the end of the east wall in case Jimmy wasn't able to light the fuse. She could only hope he had time enough to set it up before getting caught.

Josephina.

Rebekah jerked to a halt, realizing she hadn't seen the young girl during the fracas in the courtyard, nor was she among the girls Bernadette was taking to the gallery. Rebekah had to trust that Josephina was resourceful and knew what the plans were.

Maneuvering around the workshop with a casual walk—hoping the bandits would think nothing of her—Rebekah picked up her pace again and reached the broken wall the colonel wanted her to blow up. She looked around in panic, seeing nothing but empty crates. Where was the dynamite?

"Señorita Doc Beck?"

Rebekah jumped at the sound of the small voice. She turned to see Josephina crouched by a stack of crates. Rebekah came close, and Josephina grabbed her hand.

"The dynamite, it is under the crate by the wall," the girl said, her voice filled with tears. "The fuse is long. Señor Jimmy said it will last five minutes. I had no matches and could not light it. "

Rebekah squeezed the girl's hand. "You've done well, child.

Now, do you think you can get to the chapel and up into the gallery with Miss Bernadette without anyone seeing you?"

"I can, señorita. But we must help Jimmy. They will kill him when the army attacks."

Rebekah's stomach turned. Josephina had given voice to the words she refused to even think. There was no time to light the dynamite, free Jimmy, and unlock the west gate. Was there?

Josephina tugged on her hand. "Please, I will free Jimmy now. You light the dynamite and open the gate. There is no time left."

Indeed. The army should have already attacked, but they must be giving Rebekah a few more minutes to blow up the wall first. She took Josephina by the shoulders.

"Please be ever so careful and get to the gallery as soon as you can. You and Jimmy both. Call out to Bernadette before you go up the stairs. She is armed."

The girl nodded. What a brave little thing she was! Far more than Rebekah felt as she watched the girl disappear, wondering how she would live with herself if anything happened to Josephina.

Rebekah went to the wall, reached inside the dress slit, and withdrew the matches she'd stashed there with her pistol. She found the fuse Jimmy left, struck the match on a rock laying by it, and touch the tip. The sparking and hissing jolted her with the reality of what was happening.

She dropped the match, turned, and ran. She had to get to the west wall, and the gate unbarred.

She stayed in the shadows underneath the guard walkway along the south wall. It was close enough to meal time that most of the bandits were gathered at the sleeping quarters where they also ate. Rebekah dodged the adobe structure of the school's classrooms and caught sight of the gate caddy-corner from her. Directly above it, a guard stood, facing outward. Any second, and he would alert the entire gang of the Mexican army's attack from the west. Would the dynamite go off in time?

Rebekah scooted close to the wall and then crept out to go around an outbuilding in her path. She ran straight into a rigid form wearing a cream charro suit.

Sancho Guerra.

CHAPTER 14

The corn crib didn't smell as bad as the manure pile, but Jimmy pretty much stunk like one after his bath in the pigpen and the fountain. He stomped around the crib, checking to see how solid the walls were, poking his fingers through the evenly spaced gaps, and shaking the boards.

The guard laughed at him. Jimmy rattled the door, which was bolted from the outside. The man laughed again and said something to him in Spanish. Jimmy figured it was a good thing that he couldn't understand the words.

He turned toward the back wall again and halted at the sight of three slender fingers poking through.

Jimmy glanced behind him at the shadow of the guard, then edged toward the fingers. He knelt and looked through the narrow space between the boards. Sad brown eyes stared back at him.

He whispered, "Josephina! What are you..."

She put a finger to her lips and shook her head. She pointed toward the door and then disappeared.

Jimmy got to his feet and went back to the door. The clanging sound of buckets falling got the guard's attention. The man went to investigate, and Jimmy caught the flash of a red skirt by the door. The bolt slid away, and the door opened a crack. Jimmy shot out, turned, and locked the door again. He chased after Josephina, who disappeared around the other side of the corn crib.

They ran to the east wall near the workshop and took cover. The guard came back to the corn crib and resumed his position. Josephina whispered, "Señorita Doc Beck said we are to go to the chapel. We must hurry. The dynamite will go off very soon."

Jimmy grabbed the girl's thin arm to halt her. He could hardly keep up with this little thing. "You get to the gallery. I'm going to help Doc Beck."

Even as Josephina opened her mouth to protest, Jimmy fled. He had to trust God that He would get Josephina to safety and himself to the wall in time to help Doc Beck if she got in trouble.

CHAPTER 15

There was a stillness that descended over the world inside the mission.

Rebekah stared up into Sancho Guerra's face, seeing the hatred burning there. The man had shed his gentlemanly aura, not attempting to keep a coolness as he did in front of his men, and most especially his son. His look was primal, like a mountain lion whose primary instincts were to kill its prey.

Sancho Guerra's voice was a low growl, barely human as he said, "You will spend this night in hell, woman."

He struck like a rattlesnake. Both his hands clenched around Rebekah's throat, cutting off her wind. Rebekah's eyes popped, and she reached up to grab his wrists as though she could pull his hands away. That was fruitless. She needed to kick him.

She did, landing a solid blow with a point of her boot to his kneecap. Sancho Guerra puffed out his pain in one foul breath, gritting his teeth and squeezing harder.

His eyes turned red as he pushed her backward, preventing her from kicking or doing anything. Anything other than roll her eyes skyward and accept death.

The earth heaved beneath her feet as, simultaneously, an explosion rang in her ears.

Sancho Guerra's hands must have released her because the next thing Rebekah knew, she lay on her back, gasping for air and looking toward the hole in the east wall. Shouts sounded as the bandits poured out of the sleeping quarters, firing their guns toward the wall as they rushed it.

Rebekah looked up to see Sancho Guerra still towering over her, but he was watching the wall. It was rare in the twenty-four hours of being in his presence that he wasn't staring directly at her.

Before she could move, he glanced down at her, the fire in his eyes banked as he seemed to regain his humanness. He looked at her, then at the wall, and made his decision.

Sancho Guerra ran for the wall, shouting orders at his men and pointing toward the chapel. Two bandits ran toward it, toward Bernadette Peterson and her flock.

Rebekah scrambled up and stumbled toward the west wall. She looked up to check on the guard, but he wasn't there.

Rebekah held her skirt high and ran through the open space, cutting the corner as she pumped her legs hard to make it to the door. She slid into it, using her hands to stop her momentum.

With tingling hands, she lifted the bar off the door and tossed it aside. The solidness of that bar would've kept the Mexican army out for several minutes. Those were minutes the hostages didn't have now.

Rebekah threw the door open and stared across the open desert, not realizing what a relief she would feel to see open country. Nor how good it was to see the Mexican army charging on horseback across that open country.

Rebekah moved away from the door, her mind a fog. She needed to take cover. Quick.

A hand grabbed her from behind. She dropped to her knees,

using her body weight to pull away. She didn't have the strength to run.

Jimmy stood over her, both hands extended toward her. "Come on, Doc Beck! Stay out here, and we'll get it from both directions."

Rebekah let him take her hands and pull her to her feet. She stumbled with him to the far corner of the west wall that was stacked high with firewood. They holed up behind it, fortified from flying bullets and the thundering roar of the army's horses coming close.

She heard men dismounting outside the wall. Though she couldn't see the door, she sensed the moment when the first soldiers burst through.

She couldn't see the east wall, but she knew the bandits realized they were being attacked from the west. A melee of gunfire sounded, ringing high and loud in Rebekah's ears. She pressed her hands over them to preserve her hearing.

Jimmy, gun out and positioned between her and the woodpile, hollered above the noise, "You usually get in shootouts every Wednesday, Doc?"

"I try not to, dear Jimmy."

CHAPTER 16

The pounding on the door added to Rebekah's pounding headache. She had already called for the person to go away, but she received louder pounding instead.

She thought the quaint hotel room in Zapata would give her the privacy she needed that day, but someone was determined to barge in.

Rebekah rose from the bed and slipped on her robe, tying it securely around her waist and picking up her pepperbox from the nightstand. The pounding ceased, and she heard voices on the other side of the door.

"Doc Beck needs her rest!" It was Jimmy shouting.

She put her hand on the doorknob, took a deep breath, and yanked the door open. She swiveled the gun to aim it at a stranger on the other side.

The stranger dressed in a three-piece brown suit and derby hat that had seen many dusty trails. Jimmy was on the balls of his feet, telling the man off.

Both turned to where she stood, gun at the ready. The stranger spread his hands wide.

"Sorry to disturb you, Doc, but this is the most sensational story that's happened in the state in years! Maybe in the whole west. What gave you the nerve to waltz into that mission, right into the seventy guns of Sancho Guerra?"

Rebekah worked her jaw back and forth as the man produced a tablet and stood poised, ready to take down whatever she said. But what was on her mind to say would not be suitable for print.

She lowered the pepperbox reluctantly. "I have no desire for a story to be written about me, Mister...."

"Michael Hamilton, ma'am." He held his pad at the ready, a broad grin on his surprisingly boyish face. Judging from the hints of white in his brown mustache and the way his eyes crinkled deep, he was middle-aged but in good physical form. He went on, "Whether you want it or not, this is hitting the papers today. I've already sent off a lead story to the AP, and it'll go throughout the country of how Doctor Rebekah LaRoche saved a school of girls from the most notorious bandits in the territory."

Rebekah closed her eyes, her stomach dropping at the knowledge of her full name spreading cross-country. "I wish you hadn't done that, Mr. Hamilton. Please leave me alone."

"Where are you headed next, ma'am? I couldn't even find out where you live. Sounds as if you're like me, footloose and fancy-free, calling hotels all over the west home. Am I right?"

Michael Hamilton was closer to right than even he guessed.

Jimmy cut in. "Look, bub. Miss Rebekah said she wants to be left alone. I was right there in that mission, too, and what this lady went through deserves peace and quiet. Now you—"

Hamilton wheeled on him. "You must be the young hero that Josephina girl told me about. She said you set up the dynamite and clobbered one of the guards before he shot the doctor in the back. That took some kind of courage, son."

Jimmy narrowed his eyes. "I ain't your son."

The man reached out and gripped Jimmy's chin, turning his face this way and that. "By thunder, you aren't! But if I had a son, I would want him to be like you. The girl said that dynamite was old and sweating. How did you learn how to handle something that dangerous?"

Rebekah saw the shift in Jimmy's eyes, his usual glow coming back into them that had disappeared inside the mission. It was good to see. She might ask him later if one of the bandits really was about to shoot her in the back, and Jimmy stopped him. She didn't doubt it.

"Mr. Hamilton, I was in on the biggest gold strikes in Colorado when the real bonanzas were coming in," Jimmy said. "Used to set dynamite charges all the time."

Rebekah smiled, knowing Jimmy was about to take off on some wild yarn. Whether or not it made it into print didn't matter. The reporter would make up things about them anyway.

Rebekah began closing the door. "You two gentlemen have a nice talk."

They both looked at her as if to object, but Rebekah had the door closed in their faces before they could say another word. She turned the key in the lock and went back to bed.

After the battle in the mission that lasted to dusk, Rebekah had spent the night treating wounds of the Mexican army and of bandits who had survived, which were few. The army showed no mercy, outnumbering the gang three to one and with far more ammunition.

The first thing Rebekah did, though, was give Bernadette Peterson, the teachers, and each one of the girls a tremendous hug. None of them were harmed. The four-barrel pepperbox in the hand of Bernadette served its purpose until the army was able to storm the mission.

The girls were now at the local church where the priest and real nuns promised to look after them for the day while the staff rested.

After Rebekah treated the wounds, Colonel Del Campo asked her to help identify dead bandits, matching them with the warrants and wanted posters from the marshal's office.

It wasn't pleasant to see the men—ones who had respected her nun's habit, threatened her, laughed at her, and ultimately would have killed her—lying stretched out in the courtyard.

The one she held her breath for each time the colonel drew back a blanket covering a bandit's face, was one she never saw. Nor was that face among the wounded, nor among the three who had surrendered unscathed.

Sancho Guerra was not among any of these. Neither was Edgardo. Pinto Diaz was missing, too.

When Rebekah had pointed these facts out to Colonel Del Campo, he shook his head, frowning. "One of my men reported seeing three men escaping south on our own horses. I feared one of those was Sancho Guerra. He has eluded us once again and will attract even more cutthroats to himself."

The news made Rebekah feel weak in the knees, but she comforted herself with the thought that Sancho Guerra was headed south, for the Rio Grande to cross back into Mexico. It was unlikely he would set foot in the states again, at least not anytime soon.

❦

REBEKAH TOOK breakfast with Bernadette Peterson at a small café in town. It was nearly noon, but both women agreed they would rather have leftover hash brown casserole, scrambled eggs, and bacon with their coffee than lunch food.

Bernadette sipped her coffee. "I'm sorry Michael Hamilton came at you so quick." Fatigue weighed on the woman's voice, but she smiled. "He's come to our mission before to write a story. When he heard about Sancho Guerra taking us hostage, he came straight here from Oregon. After coming all that way, I understand his anxiousness to interview you, but it still doesn't excuse his rudeness."

Rebekah savored the hash brown casserole, grateful she

wouldn't be interrupted by bandits charging in on them. "It's all right, Miss Peterson," she said. "I think Jimmy thoroughly enjoyed speaking with him. After their hour-long conversation, I'd say Michael Hamilton and I are even."

Bernadette chuckled. "Quite so. And after all we have been through, dear Rebekah, I think it's perfectly fine for you to call me Bernadette."

"I consider that an honor, Bernadette."

They talked for a few minutes about the children and the future of Hope Academy. Rebekah was certain Doctor McKinnon would cover the cost of repairs for the damage the bandits caused, along with restocking the place.

Rebekah asked, "How is Josephina? Does her family live here in town?"

Bernadette looked surprised. "You didn't know? Of course, with all the chaos, you wouldn't...Josephina is an orphan child. She's been in my charge for the past two years. She will remain with me at the school while we recover."

Rebekah nodded. "She is a treasure."

Bernadette smiled. "So is that boy of yours, Jimmy. What a brave rascal, sneaking in the way he did. Have you known him long?"

Rebekah laughed. "We met a week and a half ago. But he saved my life. We are quite stuck with one another now."

Rebekah didn't know what she would do without Jimmy. The terror she experienced at seeing the bandits nearly kill him put a strain on her heart.

But they all made it out, and Rebekah sensed she should thank Someone above for that. Perhaps she would someday. If He ever answered the oldest, truest prayer of her heart.

Rebekah finished the last of her hash brown casserole. "Bernadette, may I ask you something personal?"

Bernadette fingered the checkered napkin by her plate, her

gaze on it. There was a content expression on her face. "Does it concern Doctor McKinnon, personally?"

"It does."

"I thought you might ask. Robert and I were very close at one time. He even proposed to me."

Rebekah raised her eyebrows. Bernadette laughed lightly.

"Yes, we were both young once and with hearts yearning to love," Bernadette said. "But I knew my calling was to settle down and teach. I had been asked to come to the mission here and start a Protestant school for the families in the surrounding areas. Robert respected that and followed his calling to Wyoming."

Rebekah hesitated, then pushed on. "May I ask if you ever regretted it? Not marrying?"

Bernadette met her eyes. "Robert will always have a dear, dear place in my heart. But we both know it was the right thing. I'm satisfied and filled with joy at my work and relationships in life. I believe he is as well."

Rebekah nodded. Doctor McKinnon was a kind of home and family to her, and it helped knowing more of his story. But it didn't help with the questions in her heart about another man at the McKinnon Ranch.

There was no use in dwelling on that now. She needed to do what she was sent there to do in updating the infirmary. Then she would move on to whatever assignment Doctor McKinnon sent her on next.

Wherever it was, it wouldn't be home.

CHAPTER 17

Neither of the two pieces of paper in Rebekah's carpetbag pleased her as she sat at the depot with Jimmy, awaiting the northbound train. One piece was a newspaper with a sensational article written by Michael Hamilton. He praised Jimmy and everyone at the mission for their courage and bravery and even mentioned Josephina by name. He lauded the Mexican army for taking down the bandits with the assistance of Marshal Lopez.

The main gist of the article, though, centered on Rebekah. Hamilton hailed her a hero and called her a "sophisticated spitfire." Worst of all, he used her full name.

There were people in the country she didn't want to know about her work. But the newspapers couldn't be recalled, and she couldn't fret too much over it.

The second piece of paper was a letter from Doctor McKinnon. He didn't have another assignment for her. Or perhaps he did but made the decision that she should come to the ranch to spend time recovering after her ordeals with the Baxters and then at the mission.

But Rebekah didn't want to return to Wyoming, not yet. Still, she packed her bag and was waiting for the northbound train. Doctor McKinnon had wired money for the tickets. She wrote to him about Jimmy, and he said the boy would be welcome at the ranch. Doctor McKinnon was accustomed to Rebekah bringing strays there.

After a stretch of silence, Rebekah patted Jimmy's hand. He jerked, and she laughed softly, realizing he was almost dozing with his eyes open.

"Just Jimmy, I want to thank you for what you did at the mission, saving me once again."

He rubbed his eyes and grinned. "Sure thing, Miss Rebekah. We're pals. I'm just glad you ain't mad at me for sneaking along."

"Aren't."

"Aren't, what?"

"You should have said aren't, not ain't, Jimmy."

"Don't they mean the same thing?"

Rebekah shook her head, smiling. "Go on back to sleep."

The train whistled in the distance, and Jimmy jumped up. "That's our ride. I'm sure looking forward to meeting Doctor McKinnon and seeing his ranch. He must be a fine old man."

His words amused Rebekah. If Jimmy only knew what a tough boot Doctor McKinnon was. Yet a kind one.

The train slowed, its bell clanging as it pulled into the depot. Marshal Lopez had escorted them up to the depot, and he approached them now, sweeping his sombrero off.

"Doctor LaRoche, thank you for all you do for my town and the people at the mission," he said. "Please, if you are this way again, come and see us."

Rebekah stood and shook his hand. "Gracias, Marshal Lopez. I will."

He picked up her medical bag and went to the train steps to set it on the passenger car platform. He reached back to offer her a hand as Jimmy followed, carrying the carpetbags.

Before Rebekah could board, though, a shout sounded from further down the line of cars.

"Señorita! Please, are you Doc Beck?"

A young man dressed in a dark tan shirt, jeans, and chaps was running through the dust from a car that didn't reach the wood platform of the depot. His sombrero was held in place by a strap that rested below his lower lip, shading his light brown skin. It was the tin badge secured over his heart that caught Rebekah's attention.

Marshal Lopez turned as the young man skidded to a stop by them. "Deputy Thad Biggins, this is a surprise," the marshal said. "But yes, this is Doctor Rebekah LaRoche."

The deputy caught his breath. He was as thin as Jimmy but some years older. Mid-twenties by Rebekah's estimate. "I was going to send a telegram, but our line was cut by leftover bandits of Sancho Guerra's, I think," he said. "One of them is suspected of committing a murder in my town. We've locked him up and need the doctor's help."

Rebekah's stomach rolled. She didn't want to identify yet another bandit's face.

"Deputy Biggins," she said. "All of the bandit descriptions are with Marshal Lopez. I'm sure he can..."

"No ma'am, we do not need help identifying him. We need you as a doctor. Ours is away, and we do not have anyone to do the autopsy on the victim. Would you come for us? It is very important to the case."

Rebekah glanced at Jimmy, noting his eyes about to pop out. He was surely terrified she would ask him to assist in the autopsy.

She looked to Marshal Lopez and to the train that Doctor McKinnon wanted her on.

The conductor walked by. "All aboard, folks. We're fixing to pull out."

Rebekah reached for her medical bag on the platform. It looked like she wasn't going to Wyoming yet, after all.

Dearest reader,

Thank you for reading *Mission Bandits (Doc Beck Westerns Book 2)*. I truly hope it entertained and delighted you!

If you fell in love with the main characters, Rebekah, aka "Doc Beck," and Jimmy, you'll be excited to know **book 3, *Grave Robbers***, is now available! You can order it on any major retail site or through www.SarahElisabethWrites.com.

I'd be thrilled if you took a moment to write your thoughts in the form of a review for *Mission Bandits* and post it on your favorite retail outlet and Goodreads. You'll help other readers find this series.

To discover more of my books, free short stories, and to generally stay in touch with me, I invite you to join my VIP reader newsletter. You'll receive a free copy of *The Executions*, book one in my historical fiction *Choctaw Tribune* Series. Please join me through:

www.subscribepage.com/sarahelisabethwrites_choctaw-tribune-book-one.

Speaking of history, the character of Doc Beck was inspired by Dr. Susan La Flesche (Omaha), who is hailed as the first American Indian to earn a medical degree. In continued research, my mother found Dr. Isabel Cobb (Cherokee), the first woman physician in Indian Territory, in very nearly the same years as Dr. La Flesche.

Lastly, if you're not familiar with my heritage books based on my Choctaw history and culture, you can check them out on www.SarahElisabethWrites.com. Questions? Please send them my way: me@sarahelisabethwrites.com

—Sarah Elisabeth Sawyer
Historical Fiction and Western author
Tribal member of the Choctaw Nation of Oklahoma

CANYON WAR (DOC BECK WESTERNS BOOK 1)

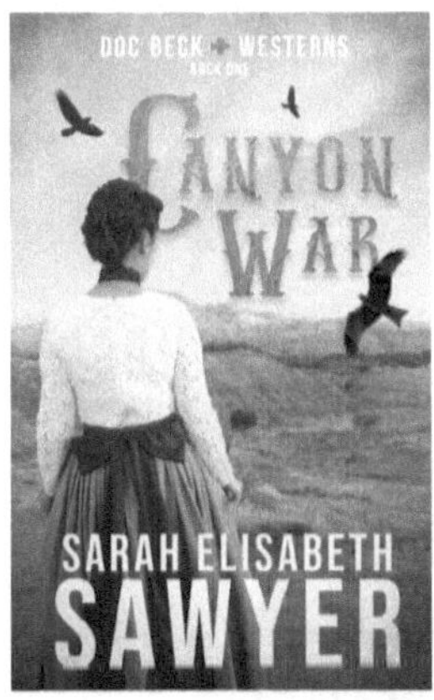

Traveling the West as a female physician, 34-year-old Doctor Rebekah LaRoche is no stranger to trouble. But on her way to New Mexico Territory, an unexpected stay in Amarillo, Texas, leads to confrontation with the Baxter clan – four brothers bred for trouble – and finds Rebekah in deep trouble.

Cattle rancher Clem Baxter's private war over grazing rights in the Palo Duro Canyon turns disastrous, and when the dust settles, one of the Baxter brothers is hurt bad. Clem sends for a doctor, not a woman, but that's what he gets when Rebekah, known as "Doc Beck," arrives at the ranch.

Now held at Clem's ranch against her will, Rebekah must plot to flee through the night with her young friend into the dangers and beauty of the Palo Duro Canyon.

Of Omaha Indian and French descent, Rebekah has always relied on her wits to get her out of any situation. But does that include facing down men willing to die—and kill—for a wild piece of land just as dangerous as any bullet?

Canyon War is available on multiple retailer sites.

◆ ◆ ◆

GRAVE ROBBERS (DOC BECK WESTERNS BOOK 3)

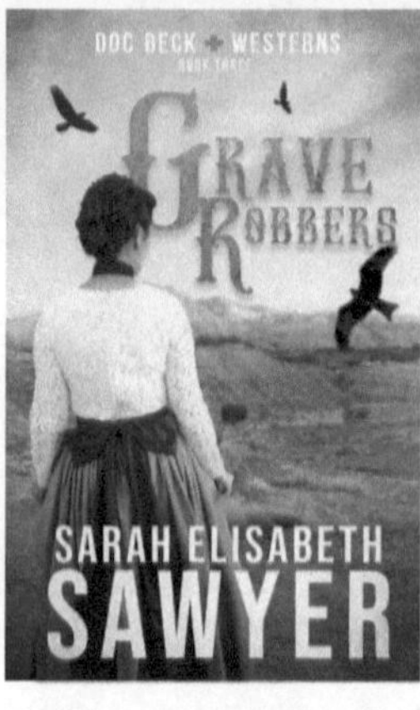

"You swing just as high for killing one as you do three."

Called on to perform an autopsy for a murder case, Doctor Rebekah LaRoche and Just Jimmy find themselves as unlikely detectives in a town with too many secrets.

One of the bandits who held the old mission and Rebekah hostage is accused of murdering Ruby Palmer, a young woman who took some of those secrets with her in death. When Rebekah discovers them during the autopsy, she must fight to prove her former captor is innocent. But she soon learns truth isn't something this town welcomes.

There isn't one straight shooter in the lot—the corrupt sheriff, judge, and leading townsmen are ready to lynch the bandit with hardly a trial. The only man Rebekah partly trusts is Deputy Thad Biggins. But what secret is driving him?

With the whole town against her, Rebekah finds herself at a crossroads:

Let the bandit guilty of many crimes hang for one he didn't commit; or prove his innocence by robbing Ruby Palmer's grave.

Grave Robbers is available on multiple retailer sites.

♦ ♦ ♦

THE EXECUTIONS (CHOCTAW TRIBUNE SERIES, BOOK 1)

Who would show up for their own execution?

It's 1892, Indian Territory. A war is brewing in the Choctaw Nation as two political parties fight out issues of old and new ways. Caught in the middle is eighteen-year-old Ruth Ann, a Choctaw who doesn't want to see her family killed.

In a small but booming pre-statehood town, her mixed blood family owns a controversial newspaper, the *Choctaw Tribune*. Ruth Ann wants to help spread the word about critical issues but there is danger for a female reporter on all fronts—socially, politically, even physically.

But what is truly worth dying for? This quest leads Ruth Ann and her brother Matthew, the stubborn editor of the fledgling *Choctaw Tribune*, to old Choctaw ways at the farm of a condemned murderer. It also brings them to head on clashes with leading townsmen who want their reports silenced no matter what.

More killings are ahead. Who will survive to know the truth? Will truth survive?

The Executions is available on multiple retailer sites.

TRAITORS (CHOCTAW TRIBUNE SERIES, BOOK 2)

"Someone's going to be king in this territory.
No reason it can't be me. It sure won't be you."

Betrayed.

Someone is tearing at the fabric of the Choctaw Nation while political turmoil, assassinations, and feuds threaten the very sovereignty of the tribe. It stands under the U.S. government's scrutiny.

When heated words turn to hot lead, Ruth Ann Teller—a mixed-blood Choctaw—fears losing her brother who won't settle for anything but the truth. Matthew is determined to use his newspaper, the *Choctaw Tribune*, to uncover the scheme behind Mayor Thaddeus Warren's claim to the townsite of Dickens. Matthew is willing to risk his newspaper—and his life—to uncover a traitor among their Choctaw people.

But when Ruth Ann tries to help, she causes more harm than good—especially after the mayor brings in Lance Fuller, a schoolteacher from New York. How does this charming yet aloof young man fit into the mayor's scheme?

When attacks against the newspaper strike and bullets fly, a trip to the Chicago World's Fair of 1893 is the answer they need to save the Choctaw Tribune. The trip holds a key to Matthew's investigation.

But Ruth Ann must find the courage to face a journey to the White City —without her brother.

***Traitors* is available on multiple retailer sites.**

◆◆◆

SHAFT OF TRUTH (CHOCTAW TRIBUNE SERIES, BOOK 3)

"Nothing to it but a stout heart."

On a mission to bring justice to the outlaw gang that murdered his father and brother, Matthew Teller leaves the *Choctaw Tribune* newspaper for his sister to operate and plunges into an unfamiliar world of darkness and danger. Working inside the coal mines of the Choctaw Nation—one of the most dangerous places in the country—he searches for a man who may have the answers to this six-year-old mystery. But after Matthew uncovers an earth-shattering truth that rocks him to his core, he must decide what right is, and what price he is willing to pay for it.

Ruth Ann Teller knows she can handle publishing the *Choctaw Tribune*—until she loses their biggest advertiser. Now, with Matthew miles away and the future of the newspaper resting squarely on her shoulders, Ruth Ann must make a bold move to keep the newspaper afloat in her brother's absence. She sets it on a course for new success or total disaster.

Striking coal miners. Outlaw gangs. An unsolved crime. And a Choctaw family that fights for one another, and for truth.

***Shaft of Truth* (*Choctaw Tribune* Series, Book 3) is available on multiple retailer sites.**

◆◆◆

ANUMPA WARRIOR: CHOCTAW CODE TALKERS OF WORLD WAR I

The day I betrayed Isaac, I vowed never again to speak my native language in front of white men.

When America enters the Great War in 1917, Bertram Robert Dunn and his Choctaw buddies from Armstrong Academy join the army to protect their homes, their families, and their country. Hoping to find redemption for a horrible lie that betrayed his best friend, B.B. heads into the trenches of France—but what he discovers is a duty only his native tongue can fulfill.

War correspondent Matthew Teller is ready to quit until an encounter with a fellow Choctaw sets him on a path to write the untold story of American Indian doughboys. But entrenched stereotypes and prejudices tear at his burning desire to spread truth.

With the Allies building toward the greatest offensive drive of the war, the American Expeditionary Forces face a superior enemy who intercepts their messages and knows their every move. Can the solution come from a people their own government stripped of culture and language?

***Anumpa Warrior* is available on multiple retailer sites.**

♦♦♦

TOUCH MY TEARS: TALES FROM THE TRAIL OF TEARS

For this collection of short stories, Choctaw authors from five U.S. states came together to present a part of their ancestors' journey, a way to honor those who walked the trail for their future. These stories not only capture a history and a culture, but the spirit, faith, and resilience of the Choctaw people.

Tears of sadness. Tears of joy. Touch and experience them.

Touch My Tears **is available on multiple retailer sites.**

♦ ♦ ♦

TUSHPA'S STORY (Touch My Tears Collection)

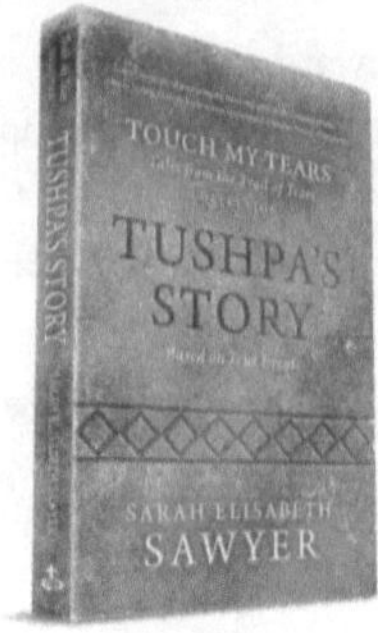

"Protect the book as you do our seed corn. We must have both to survive."

The Treaty of Dancing Rabbit Creek changed everything. The Choctaw Nation could no longer remain in their ancient homelands.

Young Tushpa, his family, and their small band embark on a trail of life and death. More death than life lay ahead.

On their journey to a new homeland, the faith of his father and one book guide Tushpa as he learns what it means to become a man and a leader.

But before long, betrayal from within and without rip at the unity of the band. Can Tushpa help keep his tattered people together? Or will they all be lost to sickness of the mind, body, and spirit on the four hundred mile walk?

A continuation of the anthology *Touch My Tears: Tales from the Trail of Tears*, this story follows an original manuscript written by Tushpa's son, James Culberson.

Tushpa's Story is available on multiple retailer sites.

ABOUT THE AUTHOR

SARAH ELISABETH SAWYER is a story archaeologist. She digs up shards of past lives, hopes, and truths, and pieces them together for readers today. The Smithsonian's National Museum of the American Indian honored her as a literary artist through their Artist Leadership Program for her work in preserving Choctaw Trail of Tears stories. A tribal member of the Choctaw Nation of Oklahoma, she writes historical fiction from her hometown in Texas, partnering with her mother, Lynda Kay Sawyer, in continued research for future works. Learn more at SarahElisabethWrites.com, Facebook.com/SarahElisabethSawyer